# Drina's Dancing Year

## Jean Estoril

### Illustrated by Jenny Sanders

AN
**APPLE**
PAPERBACK

SCHOLASTIC INC.
New York Toronto London Auckland Sydney

The illustrator would like to acknowledge the help of
Cathy Marston, the young dancer,
and her teacher Maureen Mitchell,
of the Eden Dance Centre in Cambridge.

Copyright © 1958 by Jean Estoril. All rights reserved. Published by Scholastic
Inc., 730 Broadway, New York, NY 10003, by arrangement with Macdonald &
Company (Publishers) Ltd. APPLE PAPERBACKS is a registered trademark of
Scholastic Inc.

12 11 10 9 8 7 6 5 4 3 2          9/8 0 1 2 3 4/9

Printed in the U.S.A.                              11

First Scholastic printing, March 1989

## A Note to Readers

*Drina's Dancing Year* is set in England. A few of the British places and terms you may not be familiar with are listed below.

*Covent Garden* – London's opera house, and the home of the Royal Ballet.
*digs* – living quarters.
*flat* – an apartment.
*the lift* – an elevator.
*row* – an argument.
*the Strand* – a street in the main theater district of London.
*the Tube* – the London subway.
*the West End* – London's theater district.

**Here are some ballet terms you may not know:**

*barre* – a bar attached to the wall which dancers use to maintain their balance.

*battement* – a kick.

*character* – any dance which is not done on point, such as a folk dance.

*corps de ballet* – literally means "the body of the ballet"; chorus or the ensemble dancers.

*divertissements* – solo pieces within a ballet, which usually have nothing to do with the story of the ballet.

*enchaînement* – a combination of steps.

*fouettés* – a series of rapid turns done on one foot while the other leg kicks outward to give momentum for the next turn.

*pas de deux* – literally means "a step for two"; it is usually danced by a man and a woman.

*plié* – to bend at the knees.

*pointe* – to stand on the tip of your toes.

*prima ballerina assoluta* – literally means "absolutely first ballerina"; the highest title of praise for a ballerina.

*tutu* – a short, full skirt worn by ballet dancers.

# CONTENTS

# BOOK ONE
## Drina Goes to the Dominick School

# 1

# The Mascot

London lay under a thick frost and brilliant sunshine, and Jenny Pilgrim, who had just arrived at the flat in Westminster to stay with her friend Drina, was eager to be out of doors the moment she had unpacked her case.

"I don't want to waste a minute!" she cried, shaking out her fair hair. "There's so much to see and it's all so exciting after dull old Willerbury. Besides, I can tell that you're bursting with news."

Drina looked back at her gravely, standing on one foot. She was the exact opposite of her friend in every way, being much smaller for her twelve years and dark-haired.

"Oh, Jenny! So much has happened that I shan't know where to start. Everything's wonderful! And I love London!"

Jenny looked at her shrewdly. She had perception as well as more than her fair share of commonsense and it was easy to see that Drina was happy – happy and excited, as though life were suddenly almost more than wonderful.

"You didn't think that London was lovely when your grandparents took you away from Willerbury and the Selswick School. I remember how you looked in

September when I came to stay with you. You thought everything was over and that you'd never dance again."

"Yes, I did think that," Drina said very soberly, as they let themselves out of the flat and went down in the lift. "I really believed that everything was over. Oh, Jenny, even now I just hate to look back at that time. Everything was horrible. Granny didn't mean me to dance, and I didn't know anyone in London, and I missed Madame and everyone at the dancing school – and *you*."

Jenny was silent for several moments, as they reached Millbank and waited for a lull in the traffic before crossing over towards Victoria Tower Gardens and the Houses of Parliament. Then she lifted her head and sniffed.

"I can smell the river! How exciting to live so near it. And *look* at dear Big Ben! No one could prefer living in the wilds of Warwickshire unless they were like me and meant to be a farmer or something when they grew up. London's wonderful, but I'd hate to be so far away from my uncle's farm." She took Drina's arm and they marched on rapidly towards Westminster Bridge and the Victoria Embankment. It was far too cold, in spite of the sun, to dawdle for long.

"Tell me all about it. I know something's happened. I should have known without your peculiar postcard. It made me wild with curiosity at the time, though I knew I'd see you in a day or two. Before that I was really very worried about you, practising at Miss Whiteway's without your grandparents knowing. I knew the balloon would go up and everything come out, but I expected you to be really miserable and not looking as though you could dance to the moon!"

"It did go up," Drina admitted. "It was awful at first,

too. Granny met Miss Whiteway in the Army and Navy
Stores and I thought there'd be a dreadful row. But
there wasn't really, though Granny looked so strange
at first. Then she told us that my mother had been a
dancer, and that she'd always hated the thought of my
being one, but that she was beginning to realise that
she'd been wrong. I couldn't *write* it, though. I had to
wait and tell you properly."

"I always knew she'd have to agree," Jenny said
sagely. "I told you you were born to dance. It stuck out
a mile. And we always thought that your mother must
have been a dancer."

Drina's big dark eyes were shining in her small pale
face.

"Not always. It took me years to think it must be
that. But we decided that she must have been in a
third-rate company, didn't we? Granny didn't explain
properly then, though she said she would later. Then
we went to Covent Garden to see the Royal Ballet on
New Year's Eve, and – oh, Jenny! I shall never, never
forget that as long as I live. It was the most wonderful
night of my life. In the interval we met Mr Colin
Amberdown, who writes about the ballet and has
something to do with the Igor Dominick Company –
though I don't know quite what – and he told me that
Elizabeth Ivory was my *mother*!" Though the incredible
news was nearly four days old she still spoke as though
it were a miracle in which she could not believe.

Jenny's own mother was passionately interested in
the ballet and there had been a time, two or three years
before, when she had hoped that Jenny herself would
make a dancer. Jenny, after a few terms at the Selswick
Dancing School in Willerbury, had made it quite clear
that she had no talent and no desire at all to dance.
Jenny cared about the country and about farming, but

she had absorbed a good deal of information about the world of ballet from her mother, and the name of the great dancer, Elizabeth Ivory, was entirely familiar to her. Ivory, in some ways the greatest dancer of all time, who had had so early and tragic a death!

Jenny stood stockstill at the beginning of the Victoria Embankment, with no eyes for the barges and other craft moving up and down the river. Her astonishment and unbelief satisfied Drina, for it expressed something of her own emotion.

"Drina! It's not true! Ivory your mother! Then why on earth didn't Mrs Chester – your grandmother – tell you?"

"Because she hated it all. She never wanted Mother to dance, and then, after all the years of work and having no time for any other sort of life, she got terribly famous and they saw less of her than ever. She travelled about such a lot, you know, and even when she was in London it was always rehearsals, and practising, and shows. And then Granny says she can't get over the feeling that ballet killed her. She was flying to New York, you know, to dance there as guest artist when her plane crashed."

"I can see that your granny'd feel bad." Jenny was still extremely startled. "But it wasn't fair to you. You ought to have known. I wonder what Mother will say? She'll be thrilled! She always believed in you."

"It doesn't make me a better dancer because my mother was Ivory," Drina said, very soberly.

"Well, no – I don't know. I *told* you it was born in you. I sort of felt it. It must make a difference, mustn't it?"

"I don't know why it should. It won't make any difference in having to work hard for years and years, anyway. Oh, yes, Granny's going to let me dance now.

I don't think that she or Grandfather really like the idea a bit, but they know I must. Granny says it's no life, and she'd like me to have time for fun and do heaps of other things."

"And I suppose you told her that it's the only life you want? You've always been sure. But *I* agree with your granny," Jenny said, with a sudden skip. "I want to be out and free, not shut away in a stuffy dancing school and later in a theatre. I shouldn't be surprised if I turned out to be good for you, you know. You'll always have me in the background, and you can come and stay at the farm with me. I won't let you turn into an inhuman dancing person, who knows nothing but *pliés* and *battements* and all those endless idiotic exercises."

Drina laughed rather tremulously. A great deal had happened in the few days since Christmas and she was still inclined to be emotional.

"Oh, Jenny! I hope we *will* stay friends. And I love the farm, even though it's so muddy and smells of animals."

"Better than the smell of hot feet and greasepaint!" retorted Jenny, who was every inch a realist. "But what else happened? I'm sure there's more."

"Oh, yes. On New Year's Day, Miss Whiteway came round to tea and Granny told her that my mother was Ivory and she showed us photographs and her ballet shoes. Just two pairs of them. Another pair is in a museum and the Igor Dominick Company have a pair, too. Of course she went to their school and nearly always danced with them afterwards. They must feel they helped to *make* her a great dancer. But Jenny, fancy! Fancy *me* having a pair of Elizabeth Ivory's ballet shoes! I shall keep them for always. Miss Whiteway used to be with the Dominick Company, until she had an accident and hurt her leg, and now she paints quite a lot and designs scenery for ballets. She was really surprised to hear about my mother and she's promised to keep it a secret from everyone. *No* one is to know, except for you and Miss Whiteway and Mr Amberdown, and he's promised faithfully not to say a word."

"But why?" Jenny asked, much puzzled. "Why a secret? I should have thought you'd want to shout it from the house-tops!"

"That's what Granny said," Drina explained earnestly. "But I can't. I want to get on by myself, not because I'm Ivory's daughter. If people knew they'd be thinking of her all the time, and they'd give me chances just because of her. I don't want that. You can tell your mother, but she must *swear* not to tell anyone else."

"She'll swear. She's very good at keeping secrets," said Jenny. "But, oh, Drina, people will guess."

"They won't guess yet," Drina said quickly. "I'm not going to be Andrina Adamo – not for years and years. I'm going to be plain Drina Adams. You know that Granny prefers it, anyway. She always wished that my mother had married an Englishman instead of a businessman from Milan, though I think she quite liked my father. And when I go for an audition at the Dominick School Miss Whiteway is going to take me. People might recognise Granny, and, anyway, she doesn't want to go. She says it seems like only yesterday since she took my mother. She had red hair, you know, and she was very skinny and plain."

"Well, you're not plain," said Jenny, who had always admired Drina's straight, dead black hair and clear, pale skin. Drina, she thought, looked just as a dancer should be expected to look.

"I am really. I'm little and thin and odd-looking, I

sometimes think. Miss Whiteway said she'd find out when the next audition is at the Dominick, but I suppose it will be ages before I can go there, even if they accept me. I shall just have to go on practising alone. And then I've got to start music again. Miss Whiteway says music's terribly important. Oh, I don't know how to wait! I go sort of hot inside when I think of months and months passing before I can really start learning again."

"What about the Royal Ballet School?" Jenny asked. "Perhaps *they'd* take you."

"Oh, but it must be the Dominick. I want it to be. Look!" And Drina quickened her pace until they were approaching a huge modern building which dominated that part of the Embankment. "This is their theatre. It was built after the war. When the ballet season isn't on they let it to people who want to put on ordinary plays, but –"

Jenny stared up at the building, reading the words "Igor Dominick Theatre" along the front.

"To think you'll dance here!"

"But I may not. Perhaps I won't ever be good enough," Drina said, with a faint sigh. "Perhaps they won't even take me into the school. Oh, Jenny, would you like to see the school? It isn't so very far."

"Of course. Where is it? I know you'll go there and I want to be able to imagine it."

Drina seized her arm more firmly and led her off at a very rapid pace. Very soon they had left the Embankment behind, had crossed the Strand and were making their way towards Kingsway. Jenny, slightly breathless from dodging traffic and crowds of people, gasped:

"How well you know London! You walk about as if you were born here. Oh, Drina!"

"Grandfather made me learn, but I only know the main part. This is High Holborn," Drina said presently. A few moments later she swung sharply to the right, dragging Jenny with her, and before long they stood in a quiet square.

"Red Lion Square! It's a nice name, don't you think? And look over there on that side, Jenny. *That's* the Dominick School. I came yesterday to look, so I know. They have the Company rehearsal room in that building next door, too. Miss Whiteway told me that."

The two small figures crossed the square and stood side by side in front of the large red brick building that bore a board with the words: "Igor Dominick Ballet School. Fully educational. Approved by the Ministry of Education."

"If you come here, it won't just be for ballet lessons, then?" Jenny asked.

"No. I'd have to leave the Pakington School and I've only had a term there. But I shouldn't mind. Some of the girls are nice, but they only care about ice skating and riding." Then Drina was suddenly silent, wondering if she would ever really come to that building every day, if she would look out of its windows into the square and feel it as dear and familiar as the Selswick School had once been.

She shivered suddenly.

"It's horribly cold and getting late. Don't you want your tea?"

"I'm starving!" Jenny agreed. "Though I had a whacking great picnic lunch on the train. But I'm glad to have seen the Dominick School. I do wonder when your audition will be?"

"I don't know. I'll have to work hard. Miss Whiteway seems to think I'm all right, but I haven't had any real lessons since last July."

They walked rapidly back to the top of the Strand and then climbed on top of a bus. Jenny was once more admiring because Drina knew which number they should get and where it stopped.

"I don't believe I'd ever get hold of London. I think you're really clever!"

Going down Whitehall she forgot about Drina's future career and exclaimed over the sights. A smoky yellow sunset was beginning to glow over London and the towers of Westminster looked purple-blue.

They tumbled off the bus in Parliament Square and, in a few minutes, were ringing the doorbell of the flat.

Mrs Chester, Drina's grandmother, who had brought her up since she was eighteen months old, opened the door and smiled at them.

"You do look cold! And I expect Jenny's tired. She's had an eventful day."

During tea she kept the conversation away from ballet, because she was most definitely of the opinion that it would be good for Drina to think of something else for a time. But later that evening, when Drina and Jenny were looking at books in Drina's little room, she knocked and entered. She held something in her hand.

"Drina, I meant to find this for you on New Year's Day, but I forgot. We've had so many things to think of lately and I'd put it away carefully when we arrived here." She laid on Drina's dressing-table a small black cat with an upright tail. It was about four inches and very beautifully made.

Rather puzzled by something in her grandmother's face, Drina took the soft little toy into both hands.

"How pretty he is! And how very well made. But, Granny, why – ?"

Mrs Chester said briskly, though her rather worn face held an expression that did not coincide with her

manner: "He's called Hansl. Most ballet dancers, I believe, have a mascot, and he can be yours."

"But –" Drina knelt there on the floor, with books all round her and the black cat on her hand. "I'd love to have him, Granny, only –"

"He belonged to your mother," Mrs Chester said quickly. "She bought him in Germany when she was dancing there once, and afterwards she rarely went anywhere without him."

It was Jenny's turn to stare.

"But, Mrs Chester, she – she –" Then she found it impossible to put her thoughts into words.

Mrs Chester said grimly. "I know what you want to say, Jenny. Betsy forgot to take Hansl that night she went off to America after the performance at the Dominick. They gave him to me later with – some of her other things."

Drina's lips quivered, as she held the little cat.

"Oh, Granny! She went without her mascot, and –"

"– And the plane crashed. Yes, but don't start being superstitious, please, Drina. That, naturally, had nothing to do with it. And she left it for you."

"I'll keep him always," said Drina, and she was rather silent for the rest of the evening, letting Jenny do most of the talking.

# 2

# Drina and Jenny at the Ballet

The next morning Drina, with her practice clothes in a little case, set off for Adele Whiteway's flat. Mrs Chester had suggested that perhaps Jenny might be bored while Drina worked, but Jenny assured her stoutly that she would like to meet Miss Whiteway if she was in and that she would be quite interested to see how Drina was progressing.

"Oh, you know I don't mind watching someone else," she said to Drina as they left. "Just so long as I don't have to do it myself."

And Mrs Chester shut the door on them with a little sigh, because she would have found life ten times easier if her granddaughter had been more of Jenny's temperament. If only Drina had not that absolute conviction that she *must* dance whatever happened!

But Drina herself was in high spirits as they went the long way round past St Margaret's and Westminster Abbey. There was a wedding at St Margaret's and Jenny insisted on pausing in the frosty sunshine to see the bride, who really did look lovely in foaming white and silver.

"There's always so much to see in London. I really do almost envy you at the moment. Have we got time to go into the Abbey?" Jenny asked.

"We could walk through," Drina agreed, and led the way into the great building. During the months – many of them lonely – since she had to come to London she had often slipped into the Abbey for a while and it was very familiar.

They walked softly up a side aisle, with Jenny gazing about her in awe.

"How huge it is!" she whispered. "Oh, Drina, look at the sun through that high window and the colours it makes on the floor!"

"I think the Crib will still be here," Drina murmured. "It's only January 5th and I think Grandfather said it's left till Twelfth Night."

The Christmas crib *was* still there and Jenny stood before it, her hands clasped and her face intent.

"What a nice one! I love the baby donkey. Oh, Drina, aren't you a bit sorry that Christmas is over for another year?"

"I wonder what will have happened by the next Christmas?" Drina said slowly, as they went out into the sunshine again and turned into the quieter ways behind Victoria Street.

"Heaps of things, I expect. And I'd really hate it always to be winter. Think of spring, and lambs, and earth all soft and ready to grow things!"

"You and your farm!" said Drina giggling.

"Well, the seasons matter so horribly to farmers. You and your ballet!" Jenny countered, very good-temperedly.

Soon after Drina and Adele Whiteway had become friends Miss Whiteway had provided her with a key to her flat so that she could go in and practise at the *barre* if she was out. Miss Whiteway's niece, Lena, lived with her and attended the Dominick School, but just then, Drina knew, Lena had gone home to Lancashire

for the holidays.

Miss Whiteway was not there, so Drina led Jenny into the big sitting-room. There was a note on the table:

"Dear Drina, I shall be back at about half-past eleven. Wait for me. I have important news for you."

Drina immediately went white.

"Oh, Jenny, it must be the audition! But she said it probably wouldn't be until about the middle of term."

"Well, if it is you'd better get on with your practising," Jenny said briskly. "Where's the studio! It reminds me of when Mother gave me that room at home. It's a spare bedroom again now that not even you are there to want it."

"I liked working at your *barre*," said Drina, hastily pulling off her clothes and scrambling into her practice things.

"I know you did. But I didn't. Look here! There's a piano, so shall I play for you? I think I can manage that. I know what you want."

"I usually use the record-player, but the piano would be miles easier. Miss Whiteway brought it in here because she likes to play for me sometimes. For Lena, too."

They worked hard for nearly an hour, and Drina was just pulling off her leotard when they heard a key in the front door.

"It's twenty to twelve!" cried Jenny, astonished. "And I wasn't a bit bored. You look quite good to me, Drina. I shouldn't think you'd anything to fear from that audition. By the way, I've remembered something that went clean out of my head yesterday. Daphne Daniety's people are coming to live in London and she's going to try for one of the ballet schools. Joy Kelly told me."

Drina ran a comb through her hair and pulled her

scarlet sweater straight. She could hear Miss Whiteway in the sitting-room.

"Oh, Jenny, I hope Daphne doesn't come to the Dominick if I go there! She never liked me much."

"Oh, don't worry. I bet you're miles better than her. You nearly always were, weren't you?"

"She was getting rather tall," Drina said soberly. "She was worried about it."

"Oh, Joy, says she's stopped growing now and has improved quite a lot again. But I bet you're far better."

They emerged from the studio and met Miss Whiteway in the passage. Jenny immediately admired her smart appearance. Her black suit was extremely well cut and her hair was beautifully dressed.

"Oh, there you are! And is this Jenny? The one who didn't want to dance?"

"I'm going to be a farmer," Jenny said, grinning.

"Then you'll make a nice contrast to Drina and the world wouldn't get far without farmers! Come and have some milk and chocolate biscuits, or will it spoil your lunch?"

"We're not having it till half-past one. Granny's gone shopping," Drina explained. Then, when they were in the sitting-room, she cried, "Oh, Miss Whiteway, what is it? Is it the audition?"

"Yes. Just wait while I fetch the milk and then I'll tell you all about it."

She was back in no more than two minutes with brimming glasses and a plate of chocolate biscuits on a tray, and she looked quickly at Drina's tense face.

"Mean of me to keep you in suspense! It's exciting news, Drina dear, so don't drop your glass. There's an audition on January 8th."

Drina's pale face grew paler still.

"Oh, Miss Whiteway! But you said – you said usually

the middle of the term!"

"I know. That is more usual. But circumstances just now are slightly unusual at the Dominick School. They've been having some alterations at the back of the building, which will give more cloakroom space and one extra practice room, and it's all finished, by a miracle, much sooner than they originally expected. So they are intending to take in a few extra pupils this term. Of course there are a number who were auditioned a good while ago, and they've informed some of those on the waiting list. I told them about you, and how I've been watching you work, and you may go along."

"Oh, Drina, how exciting! You won't have to wait for months after all!" Jenny cried, taking a gulp of milk.

"But the 8th!" Drina gasped, immediately in a panic. "Oh, Miss Whiteway, will it be all right? Ought I to go? I haven't been working much lately, and –"

"Of course you must go. I have great hopes that you'll be accepted. Come here every morning until then and I'll give you all the help I can. I'm sure Jenny won't mind." And she smiled at Jenny, who grinned back.

"Not a scrap. I'll help Mrs Chester or else go for a walk. It matters most dreadfully to Drina."

It mattered so much that Drina went home in a state of deepest unrest, half-excited, half-dismayed. She ate scarcely any lunch and in the end, her grandmother said firmly:

"Now look here, Drina! If you're hoping to go to a ballet school your health is of first importance, and you can't expect to dance well if you don't eat. They'll have you medically examined, you know. It won't be like Miss Selswick –"

"Oh, dear! Will they?" Drina asked, dismayed.

"Of course they will. They can see quite a lot when you exercise in front of them, but if you're at all suitable you'll have a thorough check-up, not only your feet. And you're not likely to be accepted if they think you can't stand the strain. So calm down and eat sensibly, and for goodness sake don't get more and more worked up."

"She can take me to the zoo this afternoon and forget all about it," said Jenny. "May she, please?"

"If you like. I'm rather tired today, so I'll rest. Only don't be late back. Because we're going to the concert tonight."

"The zoo closes early, anyway, Granny," said Drina, doing her best to finish her sweet.

"Very well. Now be careful, both of you. Come to me before you go and I'll give you some money, Drina."

They helped Mrs Chester to clear away and wash up and then both ran away to put on their outdoor clothes.

"I feel as though I ought to be practising every moment of the time, though," Drina said some time later, when they were approaching the zoo turnstiles.

"Oh, rubbish! You can't dance all the time. You'd do more harm than good. Come and see a few animal ballets instead! Some birds move like dancers, I always think, and –"

"Yes, but lots of the creatures will be inside today. It's so very cold," said Drina, as she paid and pushed the turnstile.

"Anyway, it's fun! I'm sorry for poor animals in zoos, but I'm afraid I like seeing them all the same. Let's go and see the lions first!"

Jenny was so lively a companion, and so interested in all they saw, that Drina forgot about the audition for quite long periods. But every time she remembered it her stomach seemed to turn over. How would she bear it, how would she live, if they would not have her in the school?

They left the zoo just before closing time and were back at the flat before it was quite dark.

Mr Chester returned home rather early from work, and in the evening they set off for the concert in the Festival Hall, where he had managed to book four good seats.

Anything at all to do with the world of entertainment or music always interested Drina and she got a real thrill from the concert. The performers lived in a world of hard work, alternated with moments of glorious excitement and acclaim. Not that Drina herself expected any acclaim at all for many years to come. She had few illusions about what her life would be if she went to the Dominick School. Miss Whiteway had told her that everyone worked very hard at their lessons, and that their progress in the classroom was definitely taken into account, as Igor Dominick believed that a dancer should have a high degree of intellect. Then, besides school work, there would be dancing lessons and practice.

They returned home by car rather late and Jenny was thrilled to see London at night. Drina, who always loved it, looked out eagerly too, but when they reached the flat she suddenly went very quiet and her grandmother said:

"You're tired, Drina. Have some milk and go off to bed. It's been a long and exciting day for you."

When Jenny had gone off to her room, Drina lingered for a moment in her pyjamas. She went to a drawer and took out Hansl and stood looking at the little cat dreamily.

"Oh, Hansl, you must come with me! I don't

suppose a mascot can make any difference really. It all just depends on how well we dance. But I think you've got to be there."

She lay wide awake for a time, thinking of that long ago night when Hansl had been left in her mother's dressing-room at the Dominick Theatre. He remained there while the great aircraft flew across the Atlantic and Elizabeth Ivory perhaps slept. Drina hoped that she had been asleep when the plane had plunged down and down towards the dark ocean.

But it was really no use letting her imagination dwell on that distant, tragic occasion and she turned her thoughts to happier things, remembering Miss Whiteway's kindness and confidence. *She* thought that there was a good chance of her getting into the Dominick School.

Thinking about Adele Whiteway Drina slept at last.

The next few days were strange ones for Drina. She was keyed up to a great state of tension and there were times when her dancing did not go well. She felt unusually stiff and awkward and sometimes had to do an exercise again and again before she could get it right. She grew paler and paler and Adele Whiteway was worried.

"You're trying too hard, just enjoy yourself. At the audition just forget that people are watching you and pretend that you're alone here."

"Who *will* be watching?" Drina asked nervously, when she was dressed and they were back in the sitting-room.

"Oh, Mr Dominick, of course. He's the Director, as you know. It was his father who left the Russian Ballet and started the Company."

"Is he the Director of everything?"

"Yes, he's in charge of the Company and the school. But Marianne Volonaise is Principal of the school."

"She used to be one of their ballerinas," Drina said dreamily, already slightly soothed.

"Yes. She's a very interesting person and everyone in the school admires her very much, though I think some are rather scared of her at first. She has fits of temperament occasionally, but mostly she is kindness itself."

"Will she be there?"

"Of course. And the headmistress of the school, Miss Lane. All the ballet staff, too. And a doctor, who is medical adviser to the school."

"Granny said that. I'm scared of him."

"It's a she," said Miss Whiteway cheerfully. "She's quite young – Dr Merritt. No need to be scared of her. You are still rather thin, but I believe you're fairly strong, and your back and feet couldn't be better. There you start with a decided advantage."

"But what dance shall I do? I haven't been practising anything. Could I do the dance I did in the play at school before Christmas?"

"I don't think you'll need a dance. The Dominick audition is like the one at the royal, where I believe they only see a very few exercises."

"Will there be crowds and crowds there? Children, I mean," said Drina.

"Not so many as usual. Sometimes there *are* crowds. But this is a special extra audition. There'll be about thirty or forty, and there are about fifteen places for this coming term, which starts on the 20th."

Drina was privately appalled. Thirty or forty boys and girls after only fifteen places! But then, though it was almost impossible, she did her best to push all thoughts of the audition out of her mind. It was just no use trying to imagine it.

It was a big help having Jenny at the flat. Afterwards, Drina thought she would never have lived until the audition without her friend's cheerful chatter and occasional oddly wise remarks. She was very fond of Jenny, for she was the only real friend she had ever had. There were three girls at the Pakington School whom she liked very much, but they were not in the same category at all.

Jenny was – well, she was just Jenny Pilgrim, rather plump, fair, rosy-cheeked and downright. Jenny was, in fact, an anchor in a frightening, thrilling world.

On the afternoon of January 7th, Mr Chester telephoned to say that he had got seats for the Igor Dominick Ballet that night.

"I know that Drina won't be persuaded to think of anything but dancing, so she may as well watch the real thing," he said to his wife.

"I suppose so," said Mrs Chester, without much enthusiasm. It was almost eleven years since she had been inside the Dominick Theatre, and then it had been to watch her daughter Elizabeth create the role of Josette in *The Breton Wedding*.

"They're doing a new ballet, with choreography by Dominick himself. And *Casse Noisette*."

Drina was immediately lifted up into the seventh heaven. It was the one thing that would take her mind off her coming ordeal. *Casse Noisette*, that she had always longed to see! And a new ballet; first time on any stage.

Jenny, who would have preferred a Western film, strove generously to be as pleased as her friend. And, as a matter of fact, as they approached the front entrance of the theatre, which was blazing with lights, she *did* feel thrilled, for it was lovely to be going to the theatre in London, with the dark River Thames swishing past on the other side of the road.

Jenny wore her blue dress and Drina the dress that she had worn for her first visit to Covent Garden – a stiff white one, with a little scarlet cape and a scarlet evening bag. Jenny admired her appearance very much.

"You look really nice, and you make me feel just a lump. I *told* Mother that this colour made me look fatter than ever!"

"You both look nice," said Mr Chester, as he led them to their seats in the front of the Grand Circle. Actually, he much preferred to see young girls in blue, and yet there was no denying that the scarlet and white made dark Drina look very striking.

Drina sniffed the warm air of the enormous theatre and felt, as always, a nameless excitement. There was something about theatres – ever since that long-ago day in Willerbury, when she had watched her first ballet in the old Grand Theatre – that made her feel truly alive.

"Mother will be pleased to know that I've seen Catherine Colby," said Jenny, studying her programme. "She's their top ballerina, isn't she?"

"She looks lovely in pictures," said Drina, who was an inveterate reader of ballet books. "She's very, very fair and I believe she's only quite tiny."

"It's strange to be back," Mr Chester murmured to his wife, and she nodded, looking, as she often did, a trifle grim.

"I wonder if we shall ever be seeing Drina on this stage?"

"You never know. But it'll be at least four years, anyway."

"Probably more than that," said Mrs Chester. "Unless she walks on occasionally. Anyhow, she isn't in the school yet."

Drina herself had totally forgotten about her audition. As the music started and the curtain rose slowly on the black and silver setting for the new ballet, her whole mind was on the stage, her whole being seemed to move with those dancing figures.

It was not perhaps the unbelievable thrill that the Royal Opera House, Covent Garden, had been, for then she was seeing first-class ballet for the first time in the superlative setting. But it carried her into another world, a world that was beginning to be more and more real to her.

In the interval she was very quiet and it was left to Jenny to chatter to Mr and Mrs Chester.

Drina had never seen *Casse Noisette* before and her heart lifted when the curtain rose on the brilliantly coloured party scene. There was Little Clara in her old-fashioned pink dress, and Clara's parents and teasing brother. In the background was a Christmas tree, and soon the young guests were all being given presents. Little Clara had her straight, bright-brown hair tied back with a blue ribbon and her face was very young and sweet. She looked, in fact, just a child, and Drina was caught up into rapt interest. The fascination grew when she saw Clara next in her long nightgown, with its high yolk and full sleeves. She *did* look so very young! How wonderful to be young and yet to have quite an important part in a ballet on a great stage.

Drina sat entranced throughout the act set in the Land of Snow, and her attention never wavered for a moment as, later, Little Clara arrived at the Kingdom of Sweets. There she sat, still in her nightgown, watching the wonderful dancing of the Sugar Plum Fairy, and Drina watched, too, noting every lovely, airy movement, every curve of the graceful arms and hands. Catherine Colby was certainly a beautiful dancer, though perhaps she lacked the personality of the great ballerina whom she had seen at Covent Garden on New Year's Eve.

The thing that somehow struck Drina most was that Little Clara, watching with clasped hands at the side of the stage, was a real, living girl, perhaps cold in her thin nightgown in the draughts there must be from the wings, perhaps dreaming of the time when she herself would dance the Sugar Plum Fairy.

Drina had looked in her programme and seen that she was called Bettina Moore, and her name was printed quite small, as though she were really a very unimportant member of the Company. Yet at the end Bettina took a curtain with the principals and smiled very sweetly, holding out her nightgown as she curtsied.

"Some day, it might be me!" thought Drina. "Some day I might be on this stage, with my name in the programme." And then, crushingly, she remembered that her first testing time was to come in the morning and that there were thirty or forty others who wanted the same thing. Unless, perhaps, some of them wanted to teach, and that seemed unlikely to Drina. It might be second-best to help others to dance, but that would mean being shut away from the theatre.

"If not the Dominick, perhaps I can go somewhere else," she said to Jenny, as they sat in the back of the car on their way home, and Jenny squeezed her hand, which was very cold.

"It *will* be the Dominick. I feel it in my bones, and you know my bones never lie."

"Gipsy Jenny!" said Drina, comforted. "I remember that other time in the field. You prophesied then. Oh, I do hope you're right!"

# 3

# The Waiting Room

Drina was surprised to find that she slept very well and it was eight o'clock when she awoke to another bright, frosty morning. But she could eat very little breakfast, in spite of the fact that her grandmother tried to insist.

"I can't, Granny! I'd be sick."

"Well, take some biscuits and chocolate with you. You may have to wait for hours. I wish the whole business was over," Mrs Chester said.

Drina wished it, too, with all her heart. She ran away to get ready and to make sure that she had her practice clothes, her shoes, a towel, and Hansl in her little case. Miss Whiteway had explained that she should wear the minimum of clothing for the audition, so that the watchers would be able to detect at once any fault of posture or bone formation.

"I hope you don't get a cold," said Mrs Chester, as Drina waited anxiously in her green school uniform. "But surely the place will be well heated? Now just do your best, Drina, and if you don't get in we'll look round for somewhere else. The Dominick isn't the only place."

"I *must* get in!" cried Drina, white-faced and big-eyed, and her grandmother sighed and said no more.

As always, it seemd to her an amazing thing that two such quiet, ordinary people as herself and her husband should have produced a great artist like Betsy and a nervous, desperately eager, already dedicated child like Drina.

As she went back to get on with the work of the flat, having walked with Drina and Miss Whiteway to the lift, she wondered not for the first time what would happen if, for some reason, Drina could not dance after all. There were so many factors that might arise during the next few years – excess height, ill health, the simple but damning fact that there was not enough talent to make even a moderately good dancer. Perhaps there was no need to worry about height, as Drina showed few signs of growing much, but, though healthy enough now, she had been delicate earlier on. As for talent or the lack of it, only time would show. Drina, she understood, had made a good start and showed some promise, but so much could happen in the formative years.

For herself, she knew that she would be glad if Drina could not, after all, be a dancer, but she realised that Drina thought there could be nothing else for her in life. It was somehow impossible to think of her turning into a shorthand-typist, a nurse or a teacher.

"I suppose she could always *teach* dancing, though," Mrs Chester said aloud, as she began to write out the shopping list.

Jenny, who had been making Drina's bed and her own, heard the words.

"She wouldn't like it," she said, understanding, in spite of her youth, a good deal of what had been going on in her hostess's head.

"It might be second best," said Mrs Chester.

"Yes, but it isn't what she wants. She wants

the theatre."

"She's much too young to know what she wants," Mrs Chester retorted tartly and wrote down "Six bananas", while Jenny went off again to put on her coat. It was no use hanging round the flat hoping for news from Drina. She had promised to telephone if there was any news, but it might be hours before the audition was over.

Meanwhile Drina and Adele Whiteway were just climbing on the top of a bus. Mrs Chester had suggested a taxi, but Miss Whiteway had said that it would be better for Drina to go part of the way by bus and walk the rest. It would help to loosen her probably tight muscles and would give her more to think about.

The morning was bitterly cold, far colder even than it had been of late. Though the sun was shining, there was a cutting east wind and most people looked blue with cold.

Adele Whiteway glanced sideways at her charge as they sped up Whitehall. Drina looked smaller than ever and so bright-eyed that she might almost have been feverish. There was a faint colour in her cheeks.

"Do you feel all right, Drina?"

"Oh, yes, thank you, Miss Whiteway," Drina said, clutching her case more tightly than ever.

She *did* feel all right in one way, but there was a curious sensation of not being herself at all. Everything about her seemed clearer and sharper than usual. Someone in front was carrying a great bunch of fluffy yellow mimosa and the scent was almost overpowering.

Her stomach felt empty and her hands were icy cold, and yet she was happy. The moment had nearly come and it was a relief. By lunch-time, surely, she would know her fate?

The words suddenly burst out of her.

"Oh, Miss Whiteway, did *you* feel like this when you were twelve? Do you remember? Do most people?"

Adele Whiteway was almost three times as old as Drina, and herself at twelve years seemed, in some ways, very remote. And yet she could remember, had been remembering ever since she woke up that morning, the day of her audition at the Dominick School. It had been a new school then, with no tradition behind it, and she had wanted to try for the Royal Ballet School, but her dancing teacher knew and admired old Igor Dominick and was anxious for her pupils to form a nucleus in the venture in Red Lion Square.

Adele had gone for her audition on a morning in late May and, in spite of the heat, she had had toothache and a cold in her head. She had almost hoped, when her turn came, that they would refuse her and then she could perhaps try for the Royal Ballet School another day.

She had not danced well and they had refused her, and she had been suddenly, bitterly, humiliated and sorry. Later, however, she had had her wish and had gone to the Royal Ballet School, and it was not for a number of years that she had come in contact with the Igor Dominick again. She had joined the Company just a few months before Ivory's death, had had a few years of dancing bigger and bigger roles, and then had come her accident and the end of her career as a dancer.

"Yes, I do remember," she said slowly, at last. "It seems to me, Drina, that somehow you're making people look back. Your grandmother is looking back, too."

"To Betsy? That's what she called my mother. I know," Drina said soberly.

"As for what most people feel – I don't know. It varies very much. You've certainly got a temperament and it makes you go to more extremes than people who are more stolid. But you can't regret it. It's the thing that may help to make you a good dancer in the end."

"But it's horrid sometimes. I often wish I were like Jenny."

Then Drina said no more as they left the bus and walked rapidly towards Red Lion Square. That strange feeling of everything being larger and clearer than usual was still with her. People's faces loomed up, were startlingly vivid, then were gone. The traffic sounded very loud; a newsvendor shouted in her ear so that she jumped; a cat streaked across the crowded pavement, its fur shining.

Drina, looking at the cat, thought of Hansl and was glad that he was safely in her case. She would not produce him, but it was nice to know that he was there.

Red Lion Square seemed quiet after the roaring traffic. In front of Miss Whiteway and Drina were a few groups of adults and children, all making their way towards the Dominick School.

"We're not late, are we?" Drina asked, in a panic, as those in front disappeared inside the main door of the school.

"No. The audition started at nine, but they're taking the boys and girls more or less in age-groups and were starting with the youngest. I was told not to bring you much before ten. Waiting is an anxious business."

Drina's wide-awake nostrils quivered as they entered the long; wide hall. She smelt polish mainly, and a

faint winter stuffiness. Obviously the heating was on. Halfway up the hall someone was sitting at a table with a list before her and Miss Whiteway, greeting her familiarly, gave Drina's name. Drina stood on one foot in a sort of trance before a big portrait on a side wall. It was of Elizabeth Ivory as Josette, and below, in a glass case, was a pair of ballet shoes.

It was comforting to see this evidence of her mother, but it still seemed unbelievable that she, Drina, was connected so closely with the great Ivory.

"Our greatest dancer!" said the young woman at the table, noticing her long, absorbed stare. "She came here, you know, when she was younger than you."

"I know," agreed Drina, and followed Miss Whiteway towards the waiting-room. In the doorway someone else whom Miss Whiteway seemed to know said:

"She needn't change yet. There's rather a delay. And it's such a bitter morning that we're sending them down to the cloakrooms in fives. No point in sitting about scantily clad, and they're most of them stiff with nerves."

"It's natural," said Adele Whiteway and led Drina into the big room, where grown-ups sat ranged round the walls with their charges beside them. They sat down close to some hot pipes and Drina put one ice-cold hand on the comforting warmth. It seemed to bring her back to reality.

She looked round very curiously. Next to her was a large, shabby woman, with a worn, good-tempered face, who was talking to a pale girl in a too short coat.

"Don't talk nonsense, Rose! You just can't be sick. Disgrace us all if you were sick here, it would."

"But, Mum, I *do*! I just can't help it."

"She didn't sleep a wink last night," the large woman said to Miss Whiteway over Drina's head. "And I'm scared she won't be able to do her best. So keen to come, too. Not that it won't be a struggle, but she's got an aunt who's quite well off – her husband owns a big garage – and she's going to help. Then there's always a chance of a scholarship, isn't there? But her dad says never mind, if she's got it in her to be a dancer. Seen it often on TV we have – ballet, I mean. And, of course, Rose has been learning since she was nine."

Drina found herself deeply in sympathy with Rose, who, though rather plain, had a nice friendly face and intelligent eyes.

"The fees *are* very high," said Miss Whiteway.

"Staggering, aren't they? But then they get a first-class education as well. Not that Rose is doing badly at school now, but it's nothing but dancing, dancing, dancing. Between ourselves, her dad won a tidy bit on the pools and he says he'll put it away and use it to help our Rose do what she wants to. With that and her aunt's money we'll manage. But she's got to get in first."

Rose went greener than ever and Drina jumped up and went to stand beside her.

"I'm scared, too. But they're sure to be nice. Where do you live?"

"Earl's Court," said Rose, smiling faintly. "Where do you?"

"Westminster. But I used to live in Warwickshire. Won't it be wonderful if we both get in?"

"I shall die if I don't!" said Rose.

"I don't mind a bit whether I get in or not!" said a self-possessed boy on the other side of Rose. "It's all Mum, anyway. I'd sooner learn to fly when I'm older."

"Shhh, Bill!" said the well-dressed woman who seemed to be his mother. "You show great talent, you know you do. And think of Nijinski and Nureyev."

"I'd sooner think of great test pilots," said Bill and, taking out some chewing-gum, began to masticate it glumly, ignoring his mother's disapproving expression.

In spite of the extraordinary feeling in her stomach, Drina began almost to enjoy herself. People were so interesting, and she liked Bill, while feeling sorry that he didn't want to be a dancer. He would get on well with Jenny!

In the distance, she could hear the sound of a piano and every few minutes a candidate, with a coat over a brief practice costume, was called out. Occasionally, too, people came back. Drina heard one woman say clearly:

"We've been told to wait. I suppose that means that my child has been accepted?"

"Well, not necessarily," said the young woman at the door. "I'm afraid you must wait and see."

"Like waiting to have a tooth out!" said Rose's mother, whose name was Mrs Conway. "Anyone would think it was me who was going to dance. I must say I sympathize with Rose."

A really beautiful and self-possessed girl of about twelve entered then, with a woman who looked like a nanny. The child wore a smart dark blue coat and stood looking round her with an air of being completely at home. She had reddish-brown curly hair, green eyes and a clear skin and only her rather arrogant expression spoilt her appearance.

"What a lot of people!" she exclaimed disgustedly, as she and her companion sat down in the corner, close to where Drina was standing. "I hope we don't have to wait long."

"Shhh, Queenie!"

"Why should I shhh? Don't be such an old fusspot, Smithy! I wish Mother had been well enough to come. *That* would have made everyone sit up."

"Queenie's mother used to be a member of the Igor Dominick Company," said "Smithy" to the room at large.

"She was Beryl Bertram and she danced leading roles," said the girl. "And everyone says I'll take after her. Of course they'll accept me. Mother says they'll fall over themselves to get Bertram's daughter."

The announcement had certainly caused something of a sensation and Queenie appeared to relish it enormously.

"She wasn't a *very* great ballerina," Rose whispered to Drina. "She only danced leading roles a few times. I read about her."

"So did I," agreed Drina. "Do you read a lot of ballet books?"

"I think I've read them all," said Rose simply and they exchanged companionable smiles.

But Drina's heart was suddenly filled with sharp regret. She disliked the look of the arrogant Queenie, and also envied her very much because she looked so assured, so confident. For a fleeting moment Drina visualised herself saying, "My mother was Ivory!" *That* would cause a sensation all right and might help her to feel a good deal better.

Miss Whiteway drew her back and murmured:

"Are you regretting it, Drina? Do you want to change your mind? After all, there's no reason why you shouldn't say who your mother was."

Drina looked into her intelligent face and felt suddenly ashamed.

"*No*, Miss Whiteway. Just for a moment I wanted to shout it out. I wanted to see their faces if I said, 'My mother was Ivory!' But I never will until I've proved myself. Honestly I never will!" And Adele Whiteway smiled and squeezed her cold hands.

"I admire you for it. But it's going to be a hard secret to keep. There'll be countless times when you will want to let it out."

"Yes," said Drina candidly. "I can see that there will. But I won't do it. I don't *want* to do it. I want to dance as *myself*, and if I'm bad then no one need ever know about my mother."

"If she could know she'd be proud of you," Adele Whiteway said. She was not an emotional or easily stirred woman, and she would never have dreamed of letting Drina know that, for just a few moments, she had most clearly remembered the face of Elizabeth Ivory as she danced in *The Breton Wedding*. It had been a face that expressed many things, but character and integrity had been important characteristics. Drina, though, so very different in colouring, was very like her mother.

Drina suddenly gave a violent jump. The door had opened again and two familiar figures walked in. One was a pale, dowdy woman and the other a fair girl of twelve.

"Daphne Daniety!" she gasped, and at that moment Daphne saw her. She crossed the room to Drina, not looking very pleased.

"Hullo, Drina! What are *you* doing here? I thought you'd stopped dancing."

They eyed each other, partly glad to see familiar faces in that unfamiliar place and partly remembering old rivalries. For at the Selswick School in Willerbury, they had not got on well and Daphne had been very jealous of Drina.

"I didn't dance much when we first came to London," said Drina. "But now I'm going to learn properly."

"So am I. I've finished with the Selswick. It's better than most provincial dancing schools, of course, but not a patch on the famous London ones. So Mother brought me up for this special audition, and if I get in I'm going to live with my aunt until my parents move. They're coming to London in March, anyway. I thought we were going to be late, because we couldn't get a taxi at first and then all the lights were against us."

She went off then to join her mother and Drina sat in silence, once more a prey to fear. Another group of four girls and a boy went off to change into practice clothes, and a few more people came back. One woman was saying in much distress that they had been refused.

"They say her feet aren't right and that she'd never make a dancer. I don't believe they know what they're talking about. I shall take her to the Royal. It's a far better school, anyway."

The girl concerned, a bony ten-year old, looked near to tears, and Drina's stomach jumped when she gazed at her. How terrible to be turned down! And yet it must happen to at least half of those present.

Time went by very slowly. Miss Whiteway insisted that she should eat a couple of biscuits, but Drina's mouth felt dry and the crumbs stuck in her throat. Would it never be her turn?

She was sunk into a sort of daze when she felt Miss Whiteway give her a gentle push.

"Go and change, dear, and take Rose with you."

Drina, Rose, Queenie, Daphne and the air-minded boy, Bill, went off together and Drina's fingers felt cold and clammy as she undressed in one of the changing rooms. But she felt better when she was ready and had tied back her hair and she did a few exercises holding on to a well-placed peg while she waited for Rose. Soon. . . . Soon now. She drank a little cold water and felt better still.

But when, at last, her name was called, and she went with Miss Whiteway into the big studio, her legs felt like jelly and her eyes seemed unfocused. The moment had come!

# 4

# Drina's Audition

Afterwards, Drina could never remember the time that followed very clearly. The studio was very light and warm and there was a crowd of people at one end. But one thing was clear and that was her first impression of Igor Dominick as a handsome, commanding figure. He was not actually very tall, but you would have noticed him anywhere. He had thick, greying hair, a very high forehead and startlingly blue eyes. His voice was decisive, but more than usually pleasing.

"This is the child, Adele?" he asked. "Drina Adams, aged twelve years and three months. Yes."

Drina found herself at the *barre* and, as her hand closed on it, she forgot everything but the familiar exercises. She did not once look at the silent group of people; if she was anywhere she was back at the Selswick School, with Madame watching quietly and critically.

Her hands felt warm again and her body suddenly loosened and obeyed her, as it had not done during the last few days at Miss Whiteway's flat.

It was a shock when – how long afterwards? – a clear, musical, feminine voice said, "Thank you, my dear. That will be enough. Come over here, will you?"

She went very slowly and shyly to the corner, shrinking a little under all the strange eyes, but knowing that the dark woman in the deep red dress must be Marianne Volonaise.

They asked her various questions and she answered as well as she could, trying to speak clearly.

"Why do you want to come here, Drina?"

"Because –" Drina hesitated. Why *did* she want to come? "Because I do dreadfully want to learn to be a good dancer."

"You know that the work will grow increasingly hard? That, later on, you won't have the time for many of the things that girls like to do?"

"Yes, I know. I don't mind. I only want to dance."

"But there *will* be other things besides dancing, you know. Do you like music?"

Drina's face lit up.

"I love it! All the ballet music. And Mozart and Beethoven. Granny's going to take me to concerts."

"And what about art?"

Drina looked blank. What had art to do with ballet?

"It's part of ballet, you know," Igor Dominick explained. "Art, music, drama –"

"Oh, yes, I see! I love colours and lighting and scenery. Miss Whiteway showed me some of her designs for a new ballet." Drina was still shy, but more at ease. Less in a dream world.

"Will you wait by the door, then?"

Drina crossed the long room, not knowing that they were watching the carriage of her head and the easy movement of her small, slim body. Her face was burning and she wondered if she had been very silly. Art! She had been stupid not to see that it was part of ballet. Of course it was. The setting mattered so much, and the colours of the costumes. Probably Queenie

Rothington knew all about art.

Miss Whiteway joined her two minutes later.

"Come on, Drina. We've to wait. I don't think it will be very long now."

"Miss Whiteway, was I awful? *Will* it be all right?" she asked.

"No, you were quite good. I think it will be all right. They seem to think you show promise, though, of course, you've got a long way to go."

Drina felt weak and sick suddenly. The strain had lasted so long.

"Oh, Miss Whiteway!"

"Cheer up! The worst is over. I believe they're serving coffee downstairs. They've got a little canteen here, where the students who can't go home in the middle of the day can have soup and so on. Miss Volonaise told me to take you down."

In the yellow-painted canteen several parents and candidates were sitting at small green tables. Daphne, who had been seen before Drina, was there, and so were Rose and Queenie. But there was no sign of Bill.

"He's gone," said Rose, who looked rather less green. "He told them he didn't care a straw about dancing. His mother was furious!"

"Goodness!" gasped Drina, awed. "I don't know how he dared. Oh, Rose, do you think it's all right?"

"They said she'd have to have a medical examination. They're not sure she's strong enough," said Rose's mother. "Strong! She's strong as a horse, except that she's off her food just now."

The coffee was milky and very hot and Drina drank it thankfully, trying not to hear Queenie's clear, self-possessed voice:

"I wanted to do a proper dance for them, but Marianne Volonaise said there was no need. She could *see* that I was a born dancer."

It sounded very unlike the rather remote Miss Volonaise, but obviously most people within hearing believed it. Queenie Rothington was the daughter of Beryl Bertram, after all.

It was half-past one before Drina and Miss Whiteway emerged from the Dominick School into the coldness of Red Lion Square. Drina's dream was to come true. She was to be a full-time student from January 20th. She was so happy that she almost danced along.

"Oh, Miss Whiteway, I must telephone at once! Granny and Jenny will think we're lost. Oh, Miss Whiteway, isn't it wonderful!"

"It's very satisfactory," agreed Adele Whiteway, and she waited patiently in the cold while Drina dialled the Westminster number and told the good news to her grandmother.

After that, they hailed a taxi and were whirled back to the flat. Miss Whiteway stayed to eat a very late lunch, and Drina, her tongue thoroughly loosened now that the tension was at an end, described all that had happened.

"And Rose is to go, too. I'm so glad about that, because she's nice. Her father won some money on the football pools and her aunt is helping as well."

"Is she poor, then?" asked Mrs Chester, who, though she would have denied it fiercely, was something of a snob.

"Yes, I think she must be. Her coat was awfully short and shabby and her mother looked tired. But she's *nice*, Granny. You'll like her."

And Mrs Chester sighed to herself, realising that Drina must meet all kinds and form her own judgments. It would be no good trying to keep her with the people whom she thought suitable. Even at the Selswick School there had been students of whom she could hardly approve, and yet Drina had taken it in her stride. But she resolved to get to know the girl called Rose as soon as possible.

"And there was a girl called Queenie Rothington. Her mother was Beryl Bertram."

Mrs Chester laughed at her resigned tone.

"I gather you didn't like her?"

"She showed off. Kept on talking about how wonderful her mother was when she was with the Dominick Company."

"And you held your tongue?" her grandmother asked, wryly amused.

"Yes. But it was hard at first," Drina admitted candidly. "She'd have been so *sunk* if I'd said that my mother was Ivory. And oh, Jenny! Daphne Daniety was there, and she didn't look a bit pleased to see me. She's been accepted too."

Jenny laughed. "I wondered if she'd turn up! So the old rivalry goes on. She always hated you because you got that part in *The Changeling* and later when you were Snow White in the Summer Show."

"I couldn't help it. She'd have looked silly as Snow White. I was sorry she minded so much, though."

"Well," said Mrs Chester, as they rose, "perhaps we can all relax for a week or two. Your troubles are over, at least for a time, Drina. So forget all about the Dominick School until January 20th."

"I'll try," Drina promised. "But I've got to have the uniform, Granny. Miss Whiteway will tell you where we've got to go."

"More uniform!" Mrs Chester groaned. "It's scarcely more than three months since I bought you all those things for the Pakington School. And I'm afraid your old headmistress won't be best pleased when she hears you're leaving so suddenly."

"She'll understand," said Drina confidently. "She liked it when I danced in the play. Oh, Granny, the uniform sounds lovely. It's grey and scarlet, and we have cloaks lined with scarlet silk to put on when we cross the grounds. Part of the school is a little way away. I didn't know that before. Or we can wear them over our practice clothes. I don't know *how* I shall wait till the 20th, all the same!"

"We'll go up to Hampstead and walk on the Heath," said Mrs Chester decisively. "I know it's cold, but the wind's dropped a little and it will do you good to get out for an hour."

"It's been dreadfully dull for you, Jenny," Drina said contritely, as they wiped the dishes.

"No," said Jenny. "It hasn't. I've been in quite a ferment all morning, and it was really interesting to hear all about the audition. What ho for Gipsy Jenny! I told you you'd get in."

"I know you did. But I wasn't sure. I was in the most terrible panic." And Drina flew off to her own room to get ready to go out.

With her mind more or less at rest, Drina settled down to enjoy the remainder of Jenny's visit and they had a very good time. Jenny learned a good deal about London. But she still insisted that, in spite of its fascination, she preferred Warwickshire.

"Think of our lovely villages, and the great beautiful houses – like Charlecote. And what about Stratford? And the woods and farms?"

"You'll have hayseeds in your hair and spend your life chewing a straw!" said Drina light-heartedly.

"So I shall and like it! You come to the farm at Easter, Drina, and I'll help to blow the stuffiness of London out of you. What'll they be doing then, I wonder? Setting potatoes, perhaps. Or spreading manure along the drills. What about a bit of muck-spreading to keep your muscles in trim?"

"They'll *be* in trim," Drina retorted.

On other occasions they went out with Mrs Chester, and at the weekend Mr Chester joined the party. On Jenny's last night they went to a new Western film, as that was the type of entertainment that Jenny most enjoyed.

Drina felt rather sad as they undressed together for the last time, and when Jenny had gone off to the little spare bedroom she stood at her window in her dressing-gown, looking towards the dark river. She knew that she would miss Jenny, though probably very soon she would have no thoughts for anything but the Dominick School and her new companions. Daphne Daniety was not likely to be much comfort, and she definitely shrank from getting to know Queenie Rothington better, but Rose, yes, Rose might be a friend.

Mrs Chester went with them to Paddington the next day and saw Jenny into the train, but she did not linger, as she had an appointment.

"You can make your own way home all right, I know, Drina," she said, and went off briskly up the platform.

"I like your granny," said Jenny, staring thoughtfully after her.

"She's been nicer than ever before since Christmas," Drina agreed. "Of course I always liked her, because she's my sort-of mother. But just lately I've felt – well, you know. Not so far away from her. Oh, Jenny! I wish you weren't going!"

"Well, I'll write as usual and you must, too. Tell me

every single thing."

"I always do," Drina said, and then she had to step back as a porter came along shutting the doors.

She stood on the ice-cold platform, with her hands thrust deep into her pockets and her face upturned, while Jenny leaned out of the window.

"Now we'd better start saying silly things!" Jenny said. "You know? Remember me to Muriel and I do hope your mum's better. Tell grandma I'll be writing Thursday if me rheumatisms's better. I always say there's nothing like a letter to cheer you up."

"And don't forget to put the cat out!" said Drina.

In a burst of giggles, Jenny was carried away into the bright wintry sunshine beyond the station and Drina began soberly to make her way towards the barrier.

She went by Underground to Piccadilly Circus and then walked briskly along Piccadilly and into Green Park. Crossing the Mall and entering St James's Park, she began to cheer up, for she always loved the familiar views of famous London buildings and the water-fowl on the lake never failed to amuse her. Here and there was a thin skin of ice, and she thought hopefully that if the frost increased her grandmother might take her skating. Or perhaps she ought not to skate when she was so soon to go to the Dominick School. A turned ankle or some other trouble would be little short of tragic.

She took so long to get back to the flat that her grandmother followed closely on her heels, and they made a pot of tea and sat down companionably to drink it.

"Jenny *is* a nice child," said Mrs Chester. "I hope you'll keep up that friendship, Drina, for it seems to me that you'll need someone like Jenny, who is nothing to do with ballet and the theatre."

"Jenny said that," Drina remarked, crunching a biscuit. "She says I ought to go muck-spreading at Easter."

"Well, I wouldn't quite say that," said Mrs Chester, for one brief moment regretting that, in spite of her many good qualities, Jenny was so downright, always calling a spade a spade. *Manure*-spreading would have sounded so much better. "But she's sensible and kind-hearted and astonishingly wise for her age. You couldn't have a better friend. She'll help to balance what I shall never fail to think of as an unnatural life."

"It's natural to me," said Drina, and ran off to fetch her latest ballet book.

# 5

# The Dominick School

By January 18th, Drina's new uniform was complete and she was enchanted with it. She adored the elegant swishing cloak with its scarlet silk lining, and the grey coat and little grey jacket and pleated skirt were very smart. With them she was to wear scarlet blouses and a scarlet cap and scarf, and if the uniform had been especially designed for her it could not have suited her better.

"I shall be starting point work soon, I suppose," she said to her grandfather, when he was inspecting all the new things. "I've longed for that. But we don't learn mime until much later, Miss Whiteway says. Miss Selswick always had a mime class, but I remember she said once it was because the parents seemed to want it. Really she didn't approve of it for very young dancers."

"No, I should imagine that the gestures become too automatic," said Mrs Chester. "You'll have one ballet lesson each morning and probably a 'character' class."

Drina looked at her grandmother with respect.

"I always forget that you know a lot about it, Granny."

Mrs Chester flushed faintly.

"You always thought I must be very ignorant, didn't you? My dear, Betsy was a great chatterer when she

was young and there was probably nothing I didn't hear about her training."

"I *wish* I'd known her!" Drina said, with regret.

"She didn't talk so much when she was older. She grew much more restrained and reserved. I suppose it was natural when she worked so desperately hard."

At the Pakington School, term had started on the 17th and on the 19th, after her practice hour at Miss Whiteway's, Drina went along there to meet her three friends, Jane, Barbara and Belinda. They greeted her with enthusiasm, seeming very interested in the fact that she was going to a famous ballet school.

"Of course it's what you ought to do. Your dancing's wonderful, isn't it?"

"I wish it were," said Drina, who was most genuinely humble and all too well aware that she had much to learn.

"Oh, well, it looks marvellous to us. We've often talked about how you danced in the play at the last minute instead of Candida Selcourt. By the way she's heard about you and she's livid that you're going to the Dominick. *She* only goes to some feeble sort of dancing school."

"Oh, dear! I hate people to be horrid and jealous!" cried Drina. She had not liked the rather older girl, Candida Selcourt, but she hated rivalry and unfriendliness. That was why she was so dismayed to know that Daphne Daniety was going to the Dominick School. Friendly rivalry would have been a different matter, but Daphne had not always been friendly at all.

"She's born horrid and you'll never see her again, anyway," said Jane. "*We* shall miss you very much. It seems funny that you were only here a term."

"I'll miss it in a way. I quite liked it," said Drina, but that one term had been so fraught with problems and deceptions that she could not look back on it with much pleasure. "But – I shall see you sometimes, shan't I?"

"Of course," said Barbara cheerfully. "You must come to tea with us in turn, and –"

"And you must all come to see me and tell me the news. Granny says I'm not to turn into the sort of person who's shut up in a different world."

But she saw that they did not really understand and changed the subject hastily.

That night she packed her little case and then spent a restless hour before bedtime. Mrs Chester took hot milk to her in bed and said that she hoped she would sleep well.

"Don't lie there thinking. You get so worked up about things."

"I'll try not to, Granny," Drina promised and, in actual fact, she did fall asleep quite soon. But she dreamed wildly, a long string of troubling experiences. She had overslept and then could not get on a bus . . . then she found that she had forgotten her case . . . she was on the bus in her leotard and ballet shoes and everyone was staring at her. When finally she reached the Dominick School, everyone else was in fancy dress and Marianne Volonaise, dressed in flowing red robes, told her that she would be expelled if she could not improvise a costume at once.

She awoke, trembling and relieved, to find that it was seven o'clock and that none of the frightening things had really happened.

But it was a relief when she was safely on the bus, then making her way towards Red Lion Square, and a further relief when she saw a little figure in a short shabby coat and recognised Rose.

They grinned at each other rather shyly and went on

across the square together.

"I'm in a terrible panic," Rose confessed. "You must think me a dreadful coward. I was in a panic at the audition."

"Oh, but so was I," Drina confessed. "I thought I'd never live through it."

"And my uniform wasn't quite ready and that makes me feel worse –"

"Oh, I shouldn't bother about *that*," Drina said cheerfully. "I don't suppose anyone will even notice."

Girls and a few boys were thronging the hall and they paused shyly until someone told them which cloakroom to use. Most of the students seemed to them very tall and confident, but in one cloakroom that they passed were some quite small girls, all chattering eagerly as they changed into practice clothes.

Once more, Drina felt rather as though she must be dreaming, but it was a pleasant enough dream. She was a member of the famous Dominick School and, unless she turned out to be a dismal failure, she would be there until she was tall and confident like the older girls.

She was pleased when Miss Whiteway's niece, Lena, who was a year or two older, found her and offered to show her round a little.

"We've got a quarter of an hour, at least. It'll help you to get your bearings. Your classroom is at the front on the first floor and this is where you'll have your ballet lessons. Most of them, anyway." And she opened the door of a big, light studio into which the wintry sun was streaming. "You'll have Miss Bower for ballet for the rest of this year. We change teachers every year, usually. And your class teacher is Miss Marshall. She's nice."

Drina listened and tried to take it all in, but it was

very bewildering. There were so many corridors and they were thronged with so many strange people, many of them looking exactly alike, in practice clothes and with tied back hair.

She felt nervous and excited and very anxious not to do anything silly. It would be dreadful to get lost in that big, crowded building, where she was so small and unimportant a unit. But Lena, who had met Drina several times at her aunt's flat, was a kind-hearted girl and she stuck to Drina until it was time for her first ballet lesson.

Drina assembled with the rest of her class and was relieved to find that Rose was to be with her, though it was less cheering to find Daphne and Queenie also present. Daphne gave her an unenthusiastic smile, but Queenie ignored her altogether. She was far too occupied, until the ballet teacher entered, in telling everyone about her mother and how she expected to be a ballerina herself one day. True, her neighbours did not seem especially interested, having similar ambitions themselves, but Queenie was not deterred.

The first ballet class was a revelation to Drina. Madame at the Selswick School had worked them hard, so she had thought, but this was quite different. Sheer concentrated hard work. She soon became aware that some of the girls who had been in the school for a good while, were far better than she was and she set her mouth and worked with a will, though without any special success.

Miss Bower said once. "You're trying almost too hard, dear. You're not relaxed. That position wasn't as good as it could be. Let me see you do it again, and remember to tuck in your tail."

And Drina did it again and again.

But she was not the only one who came in for

criticism. Rose was shy and nervous and so were several of the other new students. There were no boys in the class and Drina was not suprised, because she had already been told that they were taught separately.

At the end of the hour, they were dismissed to their classrooms, but not a great deal of school work was done that morning. Books were given out and timetables compiled and twelve o'clock came before Drina expected it.

She was to go home for lunch, but Queenie, Rose, Daphne and many others had brought sandwiches and were to have soup in the canteen. Drina went off a trifle reluctantly, but her grandmother had insisted that, at any rate in the winter, she must have a proper hot meal.

"You never eat much breakfast," she had said, "so you must have a midday meal. There'll be plenty of time, as you have a two-hour break."

Drina returned as early as she could and was amazed to find that already the Dominick School seemed a little familiar. There was no one else in the hall and she dropped a little curtsy to her mother's ballet shoes in their glass case. She was deeply embarrassed, a moment later, to see that she had been observed, for Marianne Volonaise herself was coming down the stairs, a noticeable figure in her elegant coat, with her dark head held high.

She smiled at Drina, but did not speak, and as she went on quickly out of the front door Drina turned towards the cloakrooms, her heart beating fast. What on earth had Madam – for she had already learned that Miss Volonaise was never Madame – thought of her? But perhaps she hadn't thought at all. She must be so very busy, with the ballet company as well as the school to occupy her thoughts.

Several of the girls were in the cloakrooms, washing their hands and tidying their hair in readiness for afternoon school. Just as Drina arrived, Rose went over to her coat and took a handkerchief out of her pocket and Queenie asked her in her clear, high voice:

"What's your name? Rose, isn't it? Why on earth have you come in your old coat?"

Rose flushed to her ears.

"It isn't. I haven't any other coat, but I'm getting my grey one next week. It – it had to be altered. It was too long."

Queenie laughed and turned away, saying to no one in particular that there seemed to be a very *mixed* crowd at the Dominick School.

Drina liked Rose and hated snobbery, and now she could not stop herself. She took three long steps towards Queenie and faced her unflinchingly.

"What a perfectly horrible thing to say! And who cares if you don't like Rose's coat? We might not like plenty of *your* things, but we'd be too polite to say so."

Several girls giggled and Queenie flushed. She looked Drina up and down.

"Think a lot of yourself, don't you? Who are you, anyway?"

"Drina Adams, and I don't. But *you* do. Even if your mother *was* Beryl Bertram it doesn't mean you can forget all about good manners."

By then, everyone was gathering round and Drina suddenly grew shy again. She took off her coat hastily, changed her shoes and seized Rose's hand.

"Come on! Let's go up."

"It was really nice of you, but you shouldn't. She'll hate you now," Rose mumbled. "And she's going to be important here, I feel sure."

"I don't care if she is. I think she's horrid."

"And we *are* poor, you know, really. I've had that coat for two years and I've grown out of it."

"Who cares about coats? And you'll have your proper one soon. I think she was a pig!" Drina said with emphasis.

They had art, history and English that afternoon, and the time passed quickly. Miss Marshall, who took the last two subjects, was a pleasant, youngish woman with a friendly manner and Drina thought that she would enjoy the work. But somehow it was strange, looking round at the bent heads of the other girls, to think that she was actually at a famous ballet school. It might have been any ordinary sort of school.

But she had a sharp reminder that it was, in fact, no ordinary place when she and Rose, together with a group of other girls, were streaming out into the square that afternoon. A small, fair girl suddenly seized her arm.

"Hey! Look! They're coming out. There must have been a rehearsal. There's Catherine Colby in the jeans and the fur fabric jacket. She's left her car over there. That little grey one."

"Oh!" Drina stared at the crowd of dancers in deepest interest, hardly able to believe that they were the same beings who had entranced her on the stage of the Dominick Theatre. They looked ordinary enough now.

"That man in the black anorak is Peter Bernoise, the principal male dancer," went on the girl, who had already been at the Dominick School for nearly two years.

Drina suddenly thought that she recognised rather long bright brown hair and a sweet, pale little face.

"Who's that? In the blue jacket."

"Bettina Moore. She's dancing Little Clara in *Casse*

*Noisette* at the moment, but she's really still in the school. She's one of our most promising people. I heard Madam say something to Igor Dominick once when they didn't know I was there."

"But how old is she?" Bettina looked very young off the stage as well as on it.

"Oh, sixteen-ish. She's been in the *corps de ballet* since before Christmas, and they gave her Little Clara because she just suited it. I heard they took her in because so many of them had flu in December. But she deserves it. She's really nice. No swank."

Bettina did look nice, and Drina walked away with Rose feeling that she would love to get to know her, but of course she never would. Bettina Moore, already with her career well started, would have no interest in an insignicant new student of twelve.

Rose and Drina stood outside High Holborn Tube Station for a moment.

"Do you think you're going to like it?" Rose asked. "I feel sort of muddled; so much has happened. And there are so many people to get to know."

"Oh, yes," Drina said. "I'm sure I *shall* like it. But I wish I'd been able to join the school earlier. Miss Bower didn't say so, but I'm sure she thinks that dancers from provincial dancing schools are miles behind the others. And it's true, too. I shall have to work terribly hard. Wouldn't it be dreadful if they threw us out after a year?"

"Dreadful!" Rose agreed, in shocked tones. "Oh, Drina, what if they did? We've really only been accepted for a year, and then they –"

"We'd better not think about it, except to work harder," said Drina, and she waved and hurried away towards the Strand.

# 6

# Drina loses
# her Temper

That evening Drina sat with her grandparents and described her day in great detail.

"Some of it was lovely, and some was rather awful. My dancing isn't nearly as good as some of the others, and my ballet teacher, Miss Bower, is a rather scaring sort of person. Very graceful and rather tall, with a darting sort of glance and awfully bright eyes. She seems to see just everything. I'm a bit frightened of her, though I'm sure she's nice. Miss Marshall is sweet. I'm not afraid of her. When she read my essay she said I seemed to have a good command of English."

"And did you see any of the important people?" her grandfather asked.

"Only Miss Volonaise, coming down the stairs. And the Ballet Company was coming out of the rehearsal room at four o'clock. Miss Colby was there, and that girl who danced Little Clara. She's still in the school – fancy! And she's sixteen, though she doesn't look it."

"I can see it's going to absorb you utterly," said her grandmother, with one of her wry smiles. "How it takes me back! Betsy used to talk of her glimpses of them when she first went to the school. Once, she was running along a corridor and went full tilt into old Mr Dominick. That must have been two years before he died. He was a most regal old man with a curly beard, and Betsy was always very much in awe of him. But she said he just patted her on the head and said, 'The energy of youth!'"

Drina found these scraps of information about her mother's early life wonderfully interesting. All the more so because she had heard so very little until the last few weeks. It satisfied a hitherto starved part of her to know that she could ask questions about her mother and be told little anecdotes in return.

"I was curtsying to her ballet shoes today when Madam came down the stairs. I didn't know she was there. I felt so silly."

"You won't be the first girl who has done so," said Mr Chester. "She probably thought it showed the right spirit."

"I don't suppose she thought at all," said Drina humbly. "I think she must have been on her way to rehearsal."

"And do you think you'll like the other girls?"

"I like Rose," Drina said positively. "And there are several others who seem nice. But Daphne Daniety scarcely spoke to me, and Queenie Rothington doesn't like me. I told her she had bad manners because she was criticising Rose's coat."

"What's the matter with it?"

"Oh, just old," Drina said casually. "She's getting her uniform one next week. May she come to tea soon, Granny, please?"

"On Saturday, if you like," said her grandmother, and Drina went cheerfully off to bed.

The next week or two passed without excitements, though there was plenty of hard work. Drina found herself growing increasingly at home in the big, crowded building, and she began to learn the names of some of the other school and ballet teachers. She had one short interview with the headmistress during her first week and was told that her school work seemed up to standard for her age. Daphne, too, had an interview and did not seem very cheerful after it. She was not especially clever and found some subjects rather beyond her.

Drina tried her best to be friendly with Daphne, because, after all, they were old acquaintances and it seemed as though their paths were to stay together for some time. But Daphne was clearly not at all eager for her friendship. She had soon grown rather friendly with two of the other new girls called Betty and Jill.

In one way, Drina was wildly happy to know that she was really learning ballet properly at last, and she put every ounce of energy and intelligence that she possessed into her work. But it was certainly true that she had lost ground during her months without lessons and she knew that it would take her some time to catch up with the bulk of the class.

She enjoyed her first "character" classes, for they were less of a strain.

"I never thought I was perfect," she confided to Miss Whiteway one Saturday morning, when she had gone to the flat to practise. "But at the Selswick I was one of the best for my age. At the Dominick I'm nowhere near the best. I believe Miss Bower thinks me rather bad. She drops on me a lot, however hard I work."

"I shouldn't worry," said Adele Whiteway, noting the slight signs of strain on the expressive face. "You've got many advantages and nothing faulty to unlearn. They must have thought you had the makings of a good dancer, or they'd never have taken you, and, in fact, Marianne Volonaise herself said to me that you have excellent poise and just the right type of body."

"Did she really?" asked Drina, with blazing eyes.

"Yes. I tell you that to cheer you up. The first term or two are bound to be difficult in some ways. You've had an unsettled time and been moved about too much. And those months without lessons are bound to tell, even though you kept on practising."

"I don't mind if I'm not hopeless."

"You're far from that, my child. But twelve is really much too early to tell what sort of a dancer a girl will turn into. Just do your best and try to enjoy yourself. I hear that your school work is well up to standard, anyway. I met Miss Marshall."

"You know them all!" Drina marvelled.

"Of course. I never went to the school, but I've always been about a good deal since I was in the Company. For goodness sake don't droop so, Drina dear. Twelve should be enjoying itself. Not worrying its heart out about the future. You haven't even got an exam to bother about at the moment."

"No, that will come. I'm *not* drooping," Drina said, more sturdily. "But I do want to be good. I can't bear to dance badly."

"If you worry you'll ruin your health and that would be a tragedy. You don't dance badly, you silly girl. And you've got many years in which to improve."

During those first weeks, Mrs Chester watched Drina anxiously, and always insisted on sensible food and early bedtimes. She tried to make life as peaceful and healthy as possible at home, especially as the weather in February was appalling, with snow and sleet day and night and piercing winds. Many of the girls were away with colds, and even with infectious illnesses, and she had no wish to have Drina ill, too.

A week or two after starting at the Dominick, Drina began music lessons again and these she enjoyed unreservedly, for she had a genuine love of music and did not find practising boring. A large party of the younger students went to a concert at the Festival Hall early in the term, as part of their necessary musical education, and Drina frequently went to concerts with her grandparents as well, usually on Saturday afternoons.

Life was altogether very full and never dull, though it could be worrying at times.

Drina found Rose an interesting and satisfying companion, for, once her shyness had worn off, she proved quite funny and they had much in common. Rose went to tea at the flat in Westminster at least once a week, and Drina often went to visit the little house at Earl's Court. She enjoyed these visits to Rose's family and liked her two younger brothers, who were lively and intelligent.

But however busy she was, Drina never failed to write to Jenny, and letters continued to pass briskly to and from London and Willerbury. To Jenny she poured out some of the things that she told no one else, and Jenny, in turn, described her doings at home and at school. She was very interested to hear about Rose, Daphne, Queenie and many of the other girls.

"Queenie sounds a nasty piece of work, and of course Daphne always *has* been jealous, but the others sound nice," Jenny wrote, on one occasion.

Queenie Rothington was certainly not a very nice girl, though she soon had a large following, for she was good-looking, a reasonably good dancer and had personality. Drina avoided her when she could, for she felt instinctively that they had little in common.

It would be useless to deny that there were not many occasions when Drina regretted her decision to keep her mother's name a secret. As plain Drina Adams she was, at first at any rate, a nonentity; just one of the many girls of twelve hoping to be a ballet dancer. As Elizabeth Ivory's daughter she would undoubtedly have had a certain importance. It would have lifted her right out of the rut and Queenie as well as a good many of the others, would have given her extra respect.

But Drina struck sturdily to her decision and kept her secret grimly. She did not even tell Rose, though they exchanged many confidences. She had said that she would make good without any help and she meant to do so. But it was undoubtedly harder than she had expected it would be when she made up her mind on that strange, unforgettable night at the Royal Opera House, when Mr Colin Amberdown had told her her mother's name.

Nearly all the girls and some of the boys at the Dominick had a mascot. It was the accepted thing to possess. It might be a special ballet shoe, a small piece of jewellery, or a tiny toy of some sort. Queenie had a three-inch-high doll, called Pavlova, that had belonged to her mother, and Daphne a tiny broach that she wore always on her coat or jacket.

Only Rose knew about Drina's mascot, Hansl, and even she, of course, did not understand the full significance of the little black cat. For some reason, Drina was very reluctant to display him to prying eyes. He was carried always in her case or her pocket, but when the others talked of their mascots she remained silent.

But it was Hansl who caused more bad feeling between Drina and Queenie and, in fact, after that there was never much hope that they would be even ordinarily friendly. Perhaps, Queenie sensed that, in small, quiet, pale-faced Drina, there was more personality than had at first been apparent. Perhaps she sensed, too, that they might one day grow to be rivals.

The incident happened when Drina was hurrying down the cloakroom stairs one morning. Near the bottom, for some reason, she missed her footing and, in clutching wildly at the rail, her case flew from her hand. The case burst open and shoes, tights, a towel, biscuits for mid-morning and Hansl flew in all directions.

Someone picked up the shoes and handed them back to her, but before Drina could pounce on Hansl, Queenie had snatched him up. She looked at the black cat with amusement.

"So our little Drina has gone in for a mascot now!" she said maliciously. "But how common! An ordinary black cat for luck."

Drina's pale face was flaming and she snatched at Hansl.

"Give him to me, please. He's *not* ordinary! Anyway, I didn't ask *you* for an opinion."

Queenie was two or three inches taller and had a long reach. She held the little cat high above her head and said mockingly:

"Well, ask nicely. There's no need to get into such a temper. Say, 'Please, Queenie, may I have my ordinary black cat for luck!'"

"Give him to me!" Drina insisted. "I won't say anything of the sort."

"Then you can't want him much." And Queenie put Hansl in the pocket of her grey jacket.

Drina had had a violent temper as a young child, perhaps inherited from her Italian father, and, though Mrs Chester had done her best to help her overcome it, it still flared out occasionally. Now she leaped at Queenie, her eyes blazing and her fists tightly clenched.

"Give it to me at once, or I'll *hit* you!"

"Nasty temper! You're not as quiet as you look, are you? I think I'll keep him. I don't mind a bit of extra luck."

Other girls were staring, and one or two even said, "Oh, stop it, Queenie!", but Drina was oblivious of onlookers. She went for Queenie with a will, forcing her into a corner and pummelling her fiercely.

"Give me my black cat, or –"

"Oh, Drina!" Rose wailed, in the background.

"What's all this?" asked a commanding voice that made them all jump, and there on the stairs stood the great Igor Dominick himself.

Drina fell back, horrified, but she was still thinking too much of Hansl to be shy.

"Oh, Mr Dominick!"

"I was in the hall and heard the row. We're used to temperaments here, but little girls shouldn't fight. What is it all about?" And he looked at Drina's red face, her swinging black hair and blazing eyes with calm shrewdness.

"I was trying to get something back. Something that belongs to me," Drina explained, in the complete stillness, and before that stillness had been broken again Queenie put her hand in her pocket and handed her the little black cat.

"Here you are!" she muttered angrily.

Drina stood clutching her mascot and did not know that she looked a noticeable figure. From that moment, for Igor Dominick, she came out of the crowd and imprinted herself on his mind.

He only said, however, "The bell will go in a minute and you haven't changed. Let's have no more free fights. And you, young woman!" Quite obviously, he did not have the slightest idea of Queenie's name. "Don't take things that don't belong to you."

He turned on his heel then, but looked over his shoulder to bark at Drina:

"Name?"

"Drina Adams," Drina almost squeaked, fully alive at last to the awfulness of having behaved badly under the eyes of Igor Dominick himself. *Anyone* would have been better, even Miss Lane, the headmistress.

He went without another word, and everyone began in a subdued way to get ready for the morning's ballet class. Queenie was the only one who was not subdued, once Mr Dominick had gone.

"Well, of all the wretched little sneaks! You needed to tell him, of *course*!"

"H-he asked. And he'd probably have stayed until we did tell him." Drina found that her legs were shaking and her heart pounding uncomfortably. "I didn't mean to get you into trouble, but I wanted my mascot back."

"*And* you got it. Well, don't think I shall ever speak to you again!" And Queenie flounced off to join Betty and Jill, who thought that she had been in the wrong, but who had not the courage to say so.

Drina spent a miserable day, remembering her fit of temper with shame and anxiously expecting a summons to someone in high authority. She danced badly and could not concentrate on her school work, but by four o'clock nothing had been said and she could only assume, with relief, that Mr Dominick had forgotten all about the episode.

All the same, she had a headache and still felt wretched. She vowed to herself that she would keep her temper in future, and also that she would stay out of Queenie's way as much as possible. Clearly Queenie would bear her a grudge.

"I hate people being horrid," she confided to Rose. "And it was wrong of me to fight. But she shouldn't have done it."

"She's a beast!" said Rose, all sympathy. "And I don't really think that Mr Dominick was mad with you. There was a twinkle in his eyes that looked almost amused. Didn't you notice?"

Drina had not noticed anything of the kind, but she went home a little comforted.

# 7

# Drina and Rose watch a Rehearsal

The term wore on, filled with hard work in the studios and classrooms. Drina felt that she was catching up, but it was a slow business and she often wished with all her heart that she had not almost wasted those long months from July to January. But it was no use blaming her grandmother, and she set her teeth and worked and practised harder than most people.

Occasionally, she won a word of praise from Miss Bower, which was enough to make her heart beat wildly with happiness. There was always a sort of contentment in going through the familiar exercises and *enchaînements*, but it made all the difference to be told that she was making progress, however slowly. She had started point work and did not find it difficult, and she thoroughly enjoyed the "character" classes.

There were a few things that broke the monotony, amongst them visits to art galleries and concerts. And one afternoon, the whole Junior School was taken to the Igor Dominick Theatre to see a performance of the whole of *Le Lac des Cygnes*, or Swan Lane, to give the ballet its English title.

As always, Drina was thrilled to be inside a theatre, though it was rather a different occasion from the time when she had gone with her grandparents and Jenny at Christmas. She thought that it was much more satisfying and exciting to go to the theatre in the evening, all dressed up, but all the same she was keyed up to enjoy the ballet, which she had never seen in full, though she was familiar with the music.

All the students wore their school uniform and they made a very solid block at one side of the circle. Drina sat between Rose and a boy called Jan Williams, with whom she had grown rather friendly, and she sat studying her programme so intently that it was quite a surprise when she looked up and saw that another group of girls and some boys had filled up the other side of the circle. They wore a uniform that was identical with their own, except that their caps and scarves were vivid emerald green instead of scarlet.

"Who *are* they?" Drina gasped, with wide eyes, and Jan laughed.

"Don't you really know? It's the residential school. There are about a hundred of them."

"The residential school? I didn't know there was one." Drina was still staring.

"Yes, at Chalk Green Manor near High Wycombe. *Surely* you know? It's only a Junior School. They take 'em up to about fourteen or fifteen. A lot of them are foreigners or kids who have no relations in London. Madam goes out there pretty often, and they have ballet lessons every morning just as we do."

"I'd forgotten. I believe I did hear something once," Drina admitted. "I wonder if they like it, or if they envy us? After all, we're nearer to things, aren't we?"

"Oh, we're a lot nearer. Chalk Green is away up in the beechwoods about six or seven miles outside High Wycombe. Matter of fact, I've got a small cousin there and Mum took me out to visit her one Saturday. She's only ten and she loves it."

"I'd hate it," Drina said. "It must be like being in exile. I'm glad I'm at the real Dominick School."

"Oh, it's real enough and the good dancers come to London when they're old enough. I believe Bettina Moore was one of them. She's in digs now, or with foster parents or something. Her family live in Australia."

Then the music began and Drina sank down to savour the moments before the great curtain rose. And in a very short time, she had forgotten everything but the ballet before her. As usual she was lost and enchanted, deep in that world that was wholly satisfying.

She found life interesting at the Dominick School, but at times worrying, too. And in the colourful world of ballet, there were no anxieties and no tensions. Just lovely, apparently effortless movement, and colour and music. Catherine Colby seemed at the top of her form and, using her grandfather's opera glasses, Drina was able to pick out Bettina Moore dancing with the *corps de ballet*.

Afterwards, they saw the "residents", as they seemed to be called, climbing into private buses outside the theatre, and then Drina and Rose set off briskly along the Embankment towards the flat in Westminster, for Rose was going there for tea.

"I wonder if we'll ever dance like that?" Rose mused, as they kept up their rapid pace against the very cold, sleety wind. "Oh, Drina, do you think we ever shall?"

"I don't know," Drina said. "Some of us will, I expect."

"Queenie's quite sure that *she* will. She sees herself as *prima ballerina* of the Company one day."

"But she isn't so very good. Better than us, but Miss

Bower drops on her a good deal. Sometimes I'm even sorry for Queenie, though she never seems to mind much."

"She just oozes confidence, that's why," Rose said enviously.

Then they talked about the ballet they had just seen until they reached the block of flats and went up in the lift. *Le Lac des Cygnes* was a better subject than useless speculations about the future.

A week or two later the whole school was summoned to a lecture on the history of the ballet by Mr Colin Amberdown. The Dominick School boasted a hall that would hold everyone, though it was rather a squeeze, and Drina and Rose had been told by those who had been at the school longer that there were usually lectures two or three times a term.

Drina went eagerly, looking forward to seeing Mr Amberdown again, if only on the platform. She had liked him enormously during that one meeting at Covent Garden.

Mr Amberdown's talk was very interesting. He traced the history of the ballet very briefly, but vividly, and finally, having carried them through the great period of Russian ballet, told how the English ballet had grown up. He spoke a little of what had gone to the making of some of the greatest English ballerinas.

Drina hung on his every word, deeply fascinated. She had read so much about the ballet that little of it was entirely new to her, but his voice was so attractive and his manner so alive and interesting that she did not want the talk to end.

"Of course," Mr Amberdown said, leaning easily on the table that stood on the platform, "you mustn't run away with the idea that all our greatest ballerinas showed promise at an early age. Often it was just the opposite. Sometimes they came into ballet for health reasons, and in a few cases simply because their mothers were eager for them to dance. Sometimes they were plain and awkward and earned more blame than praise in their early years.

"Take Elizabeth Ivory, for instance. She was an odd little red-haired child when she first came into the Dominick. She was by no means a good dancer, but she was grimly determined, even at ten or eleven, that she was going to dance well, and perhaps her wonderful spirit drove her on. At fourteen, she still showed less promise than many of her companions, though the basis of good technique was there. Then suddenly, she began to improve amazingly. She seemed to find her personality, and as soon as she got on to the stage at the Dominick Theatre it was obvious that she would go far. But how far no one could prophesy. You know that she became a very great and wonderful dancer, but it may perhaps be comforting to some of you to remember that pale, leggy, red-haired child, who had no idea that, in the course of time, her ballet shoes would be treasured in a glass case in this building and that her name would go round the world."

Squashed between Rose and Jill, Elizabeth Ivory's daughter caught her breath and blinked back a shameful tear. That morning, she had had one of her depressed fits when she had felt that her body would never fully obey her, and it almost seemed as though Colin Amberdown were speaking directly to her. She lifted her head and found that, as he concluded his talk, he did actually seem to be looking straight at her.

Half an hour later, as she was passing through the entrance hall on her way home with Rose, there was

Mr Amberdown himself, pausing to button up his overcoat. Drina smiled shyly and he turned to her warmly.

"So you came here, my child? I thought I recognised you in the crowd. And how do you find the Dominick School?"

"It's lovely," Drina said, very shyly. "But – but –"

"Very hard work? Well, never mind, it's what you wanted, isn't it? Good luck to you!" And he smiled and went off, leaving Rose awed and Queenie and several others gaping in astonishment.

"Do you *know* him?" Rose gasped.

"We-ll, I met him once. My grandmother knows him quite well."

Drina said no more, but she felt unusually light-hearted suddenly. Mr Amberdown was *nice*, and, after all, she was still only twelve. A lot could happen during the next few years.

Only one thing of special note happened that term, as it was drawing rapidly to a close. The weather improved at the end of March and during the afternoon break the girls sometimes wandered in the garden behind the building. It was small and oddly shaped, leading eventually to the other part of the school that was not in Red Lion Square at all. It was decidedly sooty and bare and not very inviting, but it was good to get out into the air for a little while.

One day, Rose and Drina escaped from the others, who were mostly sunning themselves on some steps, and they soon found themselves against the wall that separated the Dominick School from the small yard behind the rehearsal room.

Rose was something of a tomboy at times and enjoyed climbing, and she suddenly swung herself up on to the wall and grinned down at her friend.

"Dare you to walk right along the wall, Drina!"

"Oh, Rose! We might break our legs! Think how awful that would be!"

"So it would," Rose agreed, more soberly. "But I feel like doing something a bit exciting after that awful maths." She looked round hopefully and her eyes brightened. "Hey, Drina! I think those are the windows of the rehearsal room. I do wish we could have a peep in."

"So do I!" Drina was never-endingly curious about the members of the Ballet Company. She had seen them fairly often now, wandering out into the Square: ordinary enough looking people for the most part, but wonderful, remote beings to her.

Rose sat down on the wall and grinned at Drina's upturned face.

"Well, climb up beside me and then we'll get down on the other side. I *think* there's a chance, but I don't know if we dare. If anyone saw us we'd get into an awful row."

Drina, too, had hated the maths lesson, for it was a subject that she had never cared for at all and she was very bad at it. She felt in the mood for an adventure, so she climbed on to the wall, with the aid of Rose's helping hand, and the pair sat and stared at the rather high windows in the building near to them.

"If we could get up on to that little roof we could see in, perhaps," Drina said doubtfully. "But won't the bell be going in a minute?"

"Oh, not yet, surely?" Rose did not own a watch and Drina had broken hers. "Trouble is, will anyone see?"

They were round the angle of the Dominick School and only a blank wall faced them from there. There was the shrill sound of voices, but all the other girls were out of sight.

"Well, let's just nip up and then down again," Rose said, looking a good deal more wide awake than usual. "They're rehearsing a new ballet, so someone said. Wouldn't it be marvellous to get a glimpse of it before it goes on to the stage?"

"There'll be an awful row if we're caught," Drina said fearfully, but it was very tempting and in no time at all she was following her friend. The low roof was not so easy to climb as they had thought, but with a good deal of clawing and struggling they were up and one of the windows was easily reached.

"Do be careful!" Drina breathed, and they crept cautiously to the window and peered in. It turned out to be quite high in the wall of the rehearsal room and it gave an excellent view of what was going on below.

Drina caught her breath and immediately forgot all about bells and the possibility of anyone seeing them. For it was so fascinating. Down below the whole great Company was assembled – seventy or eighty dancers. Some were sprawled about on chairs, resting, perhaps finished for the day, but a large number were dancing to the music of a piano. They wore practice clothes and looked tired and hot. Catherine Colby's hair had slipped out of its band and was flapping untidily and her lipstick was smeared. Quite obviously they had been working for a long time and were all just about worn out.

Before Drina's and Rose's eyes was none of the magic of a finished ballet, properly dressed and lighted, but all the same there was an element of magic for both of them in that bare room. Marianne Volonaise and Igor Dominick stood near the piano, and Rose whispered that the dark-haired foreign-looking woman immediately below them must be the Company Ballet Mistress.

"Madame Le Caine – you know! How terribly hard they work!"

They were so intent on the dancers that they did not even notice that Igor Dominick was walking slowly from the room. A few moments later it was a terrible shock to hear a door open below them and footsteps on the flagstones.

Drina jumped and sprang back from the window and they both stared down, appalled, into Mr Dominick's face. It was quite Drina's worst moment since her arrival at the Dominick and she would have given almost anything, during those frightening moments when Igor Dominick just stared at them, to have been safely back in the classroom. For one thing, the bell must have gone; there was no sound of laughter and voices.

"You'd better come down," said the great man evenly. "And don't break your necks. We shan't know for years whether the pair of you will ever grace that room in there, but it's as well to be sure that nothing happens to you. Careful!"

They got down somehow, flushed and unhappy, and Igor Dominick continued to look at them somewhat ironically.

"Name? No, don't tell me. Drina Adams. The one who fought like a wild cat *for* a cat! And –"

"Rose Conway," mumbled Rose, then added. "It w- was all my fault, sir. I persuaded Drina to climb the wall. I – we –"

"I bet she didn't need much persuasion," said Mr Dominick. "Well, how did you think the rehearsal was going?"

They flushed more deeply than ever and he said abruptly:

"Well, we can't have this, of course. You must know

that, the pair of you. Climbing walls is dangerous for prospective dancers and that particular wall between the two properties is an old one and may not be too secure. I shall have to have it looked at. Besides, I should think you're very late for classes."

"I don't think we heard the b-bell," Rose confessed.

"Come with me."

Silent and alarmed, and deeply regretting all adventurous impulses, they followed him through the side door, down a passage and out into Red Lion Square. He conducted them into the school building and then said:

"Off you go to your classrooms! I'll have to tell Miss Lane about this, you know."

"We're so s-sorry!" Drina gulped.

"Are you really?" he asked, with an intimidating flash of his very blue eyes. "When I first saw you you seemed to be enjoying yourselves well enough."

Drina met his look and answered. "It *was* really interesting, but we do see it was dreadful of us. And – and to waste your time, Mr Dominick."

He gave a sudden bellow of laughter and pushed her gently.

"Up you go, both of you! I need all my time; you're quite right. And remember it's your own fault if you have to write 'I must not climb over walls to watch rehearsals' a hundred times."

Miss Marshall received them rather coldly, and told them to go to their places and take out their English books.

"I can see that you've been in some sort of trouble. You may tell me later."

"Please – Mr Dominick has gone to tell Miss Lane," Drina said, causing a mild sensation. The twelve-year-olds did not normally come into contact with Mr

Dominick, except that he looked into the ballet classes sometimes and caused consternation by watching with great intensity. It was felt, quite rightly, that he missed nothing, and even the most confident dancers were unnerved then.

The headmistress sent for them at four o'clock and gave them a severe lecture.

"You must both promise never to do such a thing again. It was very wrong and silly and I thought the pair of you were more sensible. Let me see! You can each write me a special essay and bring it to me tomorrow morning. On – England at the time of Shakespeare will do. You won't have much time to read it up, but no doubt you can write four or five pages. Five at the least, I think."

They escaped thankfully, feeling that they had been let off lightly.

"I like everyone here!" Drina said largely. "All but Queenie and – and Daphne. Daphne doesn't get much nicer. But the really important people sometimes talk to you as though you're quite human. Not as though you're flies beneath their feet."

"But I'm scared of Mr Dominick and Madam," said Rose. "I think it was really brave of you to speak to him as you did."

"I think it was really brave of you to find a way of seeing the rehearsal!" retorted Drina cheerfully. "After all, we have seen that!" They giggled and hurried off towards the cloakrooms.

# 8

# No Dancing for Drina

At the end of the term, they had medical examinations and Drina was rather anxious, for, though she would never have admitted it, she had been feeling rather tired. It had been a hard term and the bad weather during most of it had not helped. But Dr Merritt seemed pleased enough with her, though she mumbled something about "a highly strung child".

Drina didn't care about being highly strung, whatever that was, so long as everyone seemed to think her fairly healthy, and she enjoyed the last classes of the term almost more than any others so far.

Easter Monday was on April 7th and at last it seemed as though spring was properly on the way. The street traders' barrows were laden with daffodils and jonquils, and there were daffodils here and there in the parks. But the wind was still rather cold, and when Drina was packing to go to stay with Jenny, Mrs Chester insisted that she must take some warm things and very strong shoes.

"And you're to have a real holiday. Forget all about dancing and the Dominick School. The farm will be a real change for you."

She put Drina on the train at Paddington and Jenny and her mother met her in Willerbury. Drina was to

stay with the Pilgrims for a couple of days before she
and Jenny went off to the country.

It seemed very strange to be back in Willerbury,
seeing the familiar streets and shops. On the way from
the station, Mrs Pilgrim drove them past the Selswick
School, so that Drina could have a glimpse, and Drina
craned out eagerly, looking up at the rather grim
building. From one of those high windows above the
narrow street she had looked down nearly nine months
ago and known that she would never dance there
again. In fact, she had thought that she might never
dance again anywhere. And now she was a member of
the Dominick School and the ballet world was open to
her – if she worked hard enough and showed sufficient
talent.

"Granny says I'm to forget all about ballet," she
remarked, and Jenny laughed.

"Never worry, Drina! *I'll* soon make you forget it,
now that you've crawled out of your half-lit magic
world."

"There's nothing particularly half-lit and magic about
the Dominick!" Drina argued indignantly. "It's really a
very down-to-earth sort of place."

"Well, you know what I mean. Ballet just isn't quite
real."

"It only looks like that to people right outside," Drina
said, with sudden shrewdness. "I know what you
mean, of course. I feel it myself every time the curtain
goes up."

"Anyway, the farm will do you good. Do you know
there are kittens and baby chickens, and several calves,
and even a foal."

"But she must talk about her dancing a little at first,"
said Mrs Pilgrim, who had been looking with some
curiosity at the guest while she waited for the traffic

lights to change. "I can't say, 'How you've grown, Drina!' because you haven't. Or only about a quarter of an inch."

"I don't *want* to grow," answered Drina, with a faint shiver. "Do you know, there were two girls last term who were told it was no use going on. They'd grown dreadfully tall, and one is perfectly beautiful and a good dancer."

"I know. It's a tragedy when that happens," Mrs Pilgrim agreed.

"They cried. They just came down to the cloakrooms and cried their eyes out. I felt dreadful and so did everyone else. It's the sort of thing that might happen to anyone."

"Well, not quite. It's partly a matter of heredity, I suppose, and bone structure. It certainly won't happen to you. You're positively tiny for twelve. Do you like the Dominick?"

"Oh, I love it!" Drina said eagerly. "Most of it. And I think my dancing got better after half-term."

"You sound as though you were hopeless before."

"Oh, well, I wasn't very good. I'd lost a lot of time."

"And no one there knows who you are?" Mrs Pilgrim's face was gentle. It still staggered her that little Drina Adams, who she had helped to send to the Selswick School, was Ivory's daughter.

"Only Mr Colin Amberdown and he's not really *there*. He's a friend of Mr Dominick."

"And I suppose you never see the great man? Or only in the distance."

"Oh, yes, she does!" cried Jenny, who had eagerly read her friend's story of both encounters. "I told you, Mum. He caught her fighting with a horrible girl called Queenie, and another time she and Rose were on a roof watching a rehearsal."

"Then they deserved to get into trouble! Well, here we are at home, and all the boys will be in for tea."

It felt very strange to be back in Jenny's home and Drina was shy of the boys at first, but she soon fell into her old cheerful relationship with the younger ones. Philip, the eldest, had grown very tall and seemed to her almost grown up. He would be eighteen next birthday and was going to London to study medicine in October.

"Perhaps I'll see you sometimes, black-haired scrap!" he said, grinning at her across the tea table.

"You could come to tea," Drina said, very shyly. "But I don't expect you'd like to."

"I don't know why not. I might be really glad of a square meal. I shall be in digs, you know, or I think so."

"Drina will ask her grandmother to get you a slap up meal," said his mother cheerfully. "And perhaps they'll take you to the ballet with them. Drina knows everyone in the Dominick Company. She ought to be an interesting companion."

"Oh, I don't!" Drina said hastily. "Just a few of them by sight."

"I thought you'd introduce me to Catherine Colby!" Philip teased.

"One day perhaps she will. Look Drina, have some of this special jelly, and take no notice of him. He's getting a bit big for his boots."

That evening, Joy Kelly came round to see Drina, having been invited by Jenny, and Drina thoroughly enjoyed hearing all the gossip about the Selswick School, which Joy still attended. Altogether it was a cheerful evening, and by the time that Drina went to bed – in the little room where she used to practise, now a spare room – it seemed more like days than just a few hours since she had left London.

A day or two later, Mrs Pilgrim packed the two girls into the car with their suitcases and whirled them away into the green Warwickshire countryside, where the trees were in brilliant leaf and there were flowers in the cottage gardens. Occasionally, they passed great masses of starry blackthorns and cherry blossom was coming out in the orchards.

"How I adore the spring!" cried Jenny. "What about that muck-spreading, Drina?"

"She's not going to do anything of the kind," said Mrs Pilgrim indignantly.

"Jenny's only teasing," said Drina.

The farm was just as it had always been: an ancient brick and half-timbered structure, surrounded by orchards and backed by woods where the first cuckoos were calling. A mile away from the picturesque village where Drina and Jenny had often walked and cycled to buy stamps or sweets.

Drina sniffed the sharp, sweet air and sighed.

"It's lovely to be back in the country! I adore London, but sometimes I do like to be where the air smells heavenly."

Jenny's uncle and aunt greeted them warmly and they all had tea in the big farmhouse kitchen. Then Mrs Pilgrim returned to Willerbury and Jenny and Drina went out to watch the milking – Jenny, in fact, did more than watch – and then to see all the young things on the farm.

The kittens were mostly smoke-grey and were so delicious that Drina could hardly bear to leave them, even to go and look at the leggy foal with his mother in the River Meadow.

"Oh, if only I could have a kitten of my own!"

"Auntie'll give you one. Only too glad," said Jenny.

"But you know I can't. Our flat is a 'no animals, no babies' sort of place. Hateful, horrible people who make the rules!"

"Oh, well, christen one and ask Auntie if she'll keep it. I know she means to keep at least one. Then it can be yours whenever you come."

Drina, after much thought, chose the one with a few pretty black markings, and announced that it was going to be called Esmeralda.

"Oh, goodness!" cried Jenny, giggling. "What a silly name! And I'm not even sure it's a she. Why not call it Tiger or something like that."

"Esmeralda," said Drina firmly. "It's a ballet."

"*Is* it? I've never heard of it. I might have known!" Jenny groaned.

"Yes, I think so, but I've never seen it."

"Oh, well, have it your own way, but of course the poor little thing will get called Kitty."

"You *asked* me to christen one," said Drina with dignity, and was much relieved when Jenny's aunt promised to keep Esmeralda and even said that she liked the name, though perhaps it was rather long for such a small kitten.

It was really a lovely time and London seemed very far away. The Dominick School seemed like something that Drina had dreamed about, and nothing just then was real but the sharp April air, the long conversations with Jenny, the walks in the woods and the long rides on borrowed bicycles.

Drina forgot to be tired and developed a faint colour, and Jenny said triumphantly one day, "I believe you're beginning to agree with me about the country! You look tons better than when you came."

"It's lovely now," Drina admitted. "But I wouldn't want to be away from London for long. Why, Jenny, I go back to the Dominick for dancing lessons on the 16th. Then we go properly on the 22nd."

But Drina was destined not to go back to the Dominick School on the 16th.

The weather turned very showery and cold, and one afternoon when Drina and Jenny were out cycling they got caught in a real downpour. They had raincoats with them, but they were not enough to keep out the really heavy rain and by the time they reached the farm they were both soaking wet and very cold. Jenny, much more sturdy than Drina, was all right after a hot bath and a hot drink, but Drina continued to shiver, and by next day, the day she was going home to London, she had a bad cold in her head.

Mrs Pilgrim was very distressed when she came to collect them early in the morning.

"I don't know what Mrs Chester will say. And I thought that Drina would be so much better, too."

"I was fine," said Drina, with a slight snuffle. "It's nothing, anyway. It's sure to go."

But the cold did not go. By the time that the train drew into Paddington Drina was shivery again and feverish, and her grandmother took one look at her and cried, "Good heavens! I shall have to get you to bed. How did you get like this, Drina?"

Drina told miserably about getting wet, and how she had grown much worse since leaving Willerbury, and Mrs Chester shook her head and bundled her into a taxi.

Drina was very glad to get into bed, with a hot water bottle, but she was worried, too.

"But, Granny, it's the 14th today, and I go back to the Dominick the day after tomorrow!" she croaked.

Mrs Chester looked at her flushed face and said, "Well, I've sent for the doctor. He'd better see you. And, after all, you only go back for dancing on the 16th. School doesn't start for nearly another week."

"But it's the dancing I mustn't miss!" cried poor Drina on a cracked note. "I *can't* get behind! Oh, Granny!"

"Well, it won't help if you get worked up. Lie quiet and wait until the doctor comes."

When the doctor came that evening, he shook his head.

"I'm afraid it looks like flu. There's a good deal about. Got wet, you say? Well, she'll not get wet again for a few days. Keep her warm and she mustn't dream of getting up until I call again. I'll come on Thursday unless you telephone me."

"But Thursday is the 17th!" Drina gasped, peering at him over the sheet.

"So it is. What of it?" he asked.

"I've got to – to go back to my ballet school on Wednesday."

"Well, I'm sorry, my child, but you won't be able to go. Now settle down and get a good sleep. It's no use worrying and it's not a matter of life and death, is it?"

"To me," Drina croaked.

"Rubbish! What does it matter if you miss a week's dancing? Soon catch up." And he went off.

"It's worse, almost, than when I got mumps just before the Summer Show!" Drina groaned, as the doctor's somewhat unsympathetic back disappeared. And certainly she felt very wretched and upset.

It was awful to think of Rose and all the others being back for their ballet lessons, while she lay in bed. But the next day, she felt so ill that she didn't really care any more and was just glad to cuddle a hot water bottle and not talk much at all.

On the 16th, Mrs Chester called the doctor in again and he was concerned by Drina's high temperture. He left something that would help bring it down, and said privately to Mrs Chester:

"That child won't get back to school for two or three weeks, at least. This will pull her down, and I understand that ballet students have a very hard life. This wretched weather won't help either. It's to be hoped it's soon warmer."

Mrs Pilgrim, who had telephoned to ask if Drina got home safely, was much distressed to hear that she was ill, and Jenny wrote a frantically apologetic letter.

"It was all my fault that we went out that afternoon! I know how bad you'll feel over missing any of your ballet lessons and it must be dreadful for you. Oh, Drina, I hope you forgive me!" And the letter was followed by a parcel of small presents – sweets, a puzzle, magazines and so on. Drina was enchanted to receive it, because she was feeling a trifle better by then, though still very shaky and miserable. She did not blame Jenny in the least for her illness, but she did look back with regret to that wet afternoon when they had gone so far on the bicycles. None of her troubles would have happened if they had stayed about the farm.

"But what will they *say* at the Dominick?" she wailed, when she could speak properly again. "Oh, Granny, they'll think it so awful of me! We're *supposed* to go back for our ballet lessons, and now school's started properly and I'm not there."

"They won't say anything, except that they're sorry," said Mrs Chester briskly. "I spoke to Miss Lane on the telephone and she told me to tell you that she hopes you're soon better. You aren't the first girl to be away by a long chalk. There were plenty down with colds and flu last term."

"But some of them could afford to miss classes. *I* can't!" Drina said, in a wobbly voice. "I meant to work and work this term!"

"Well, you can please me by making the best of things and not allowing yourself to get worse through worry. It's just as I always said: this ballet business gives a child an unnatural life. It's ridiculous and unfair for a girl of twelve to have to worry her heart out about working hard."

"Fancy having to go through it all again!" she cried ruefully to her husband that night. "I'd steeled myself to it, but I knew we'd have times like this. It was just the same with Betsy. There was no calming her that time she sprained her ankle and had to lie up, and life was a misery if ever she was ill at all."

"Well, it's the way things are, and we'll have to make the best of them," her husband said philosophically. "And you must hand it to Drina that she never wavers. She knows what she wants, and she knows that only hard work will get it for her."

"She ought still to be playing with dolls!" said Mrs Chester fiercely.

"Oh, come! She'll be thirteen in the autumn. Many

girls of thirteen are almost grown up. She's very childish in some ways."

As soon as Drina was properly convalescent, she was allowed visitors and Rose was the first to arrive after school one day. She poured out a flood of school gossip and was deeply sympathetic over Drina's ill fortune.

"I miss you horribly, too. It's not nearly such fun without you."

Drina listened wistfully to Rose's tales of what had gone on in the dancing classes. How Daphne and Queenie seemed to be improving a great deal, and how Rose herself still could not quite master certain exercises.

"And Jill tied her ballet shoe wrongly and hurt her foot. There was quite a fuss. Oh, and we had a lecture on 'Art in Relation to Ballet' or something like that. Parts of it were interesting, but there was a lot I didn't understand and I know my essay afterwards was awful."

Several other girls came on different occasions and Jan Williams arrived somewhat bashfully at the flat one Saturday afternoon, carrying a large box of chocolates for the invalid.

"The first boyfriend," said Mr Chester, when Jan had gone, and he gently pulled Drina's hair.

And Drina laughed.

"Of course he isn't. But he *is* nice. Most of the boys keep rather aloof, but he's got sisters and girl cousins and he's always been friendly. Oh, Grandfather, *when* can I go back?"

"When you're quite fit. We're thinking of taking you down to the South Coast for a long weekend. How would you like to see Rye again?"

"I'd like it in a way," Drina said sadly. "But all I *really* want is to get back to the Dominick."

# 9

# Dancing
# in the Mountains

They went down to Rye by car and Drina walked over the wide, windswept reaches of Romney Marsh again. She looked over the blue Channel to where France lay beyond the haze, and the strong air brought faint colour into her cheeks.

Once, when she was quite alone in the wide expanse of marsh and sea, she flung off her anorak and danced, raising her face to the vast sky, and life seemed to be flowing back into her limbs. She no longer looked and felt as though she had been ill, though she was still thinner than usual.

It was, in the end, just after the middle of May before she went back to the Dominick, and she found, as she had expected, that she had fallen behind. It was good to be back at the *barre*, good to be in the thick of things once more, hearing gossip about the Company, seeing the important Senior students hurrying about with their cloaks swishing back from their practice clothes. But she was convinced that she would not easily catch up with her contemporaries and the feeling oppressed her.

One day, Miss Bower kept her back after a ballet class and asked her if there was anything the matter.

Drina stood on one foot and looked at her shyly.

"No-o. Only that I missed so much and I – I feel I'm not getting on as I should. I do practise hard, too."

And the teacher put her hand very kindly on Drina's rather bony shoulder.

"I know you work hard. And there's really nothing to worry about. Your point work is quite good and the rest will come. Don't get depressed about it.

Drina was somewhat heartened at the time, for it did not sound as though she was shortly to be sent away from the school as hopeless, but, as May turned into June and June passed quickly into July, she seemed always to be struggling against time, trying to make up the work she had missed.

Of course there were things that she enjoyed. Lessons on the whole came easily to her and she took a fairly high place in her class. Far higher than Daphne, who was certainly not studious, but not so high as Queenie, who dealt with everything in a dashing and, on the whole, intelligent way and who was determined that Beryl Bertram's daughter should shine. Queenie could have had an attractive personality, for she was good-looking and lively, but there was just something that prevented her from being really popular. She talked too much about her mother and was altogether too sure of herself. There were many who would have been glad if she had been taken down a peg or two occasionally.

Drina enjoyed the gossipy periods in the garden on warm days and the times when they caught glimpses of the members of the Company. She did not have any further encounters with Igor Dominick, though he often unnerved her by dropping in to watch classes.

Madam, of course, was ever present and even the youngest child in the school was conscious of her dominant personality. She was constantly to be seen about the building and she, too, often watched classes, but Drina never spoke to her and was glad. Marianne Volonaise filled her with awe and wonder; a remote being who could not come down to the level of the unimportant Juniors.

Then the Ballet Company went off on a provincial tour and were to be seen no more in Red Lion Square. They were to dance in Birmingham, Manchester, Liverpool and Glasgow, then, finally, at the Edinburgh Festival, and there were several notices about their performances in the newspapers, which Drina read avidly. She knew most of their names now and was conversant with the names, at least, of their entire repertoire.

"How strange to go on tour!" she said to Rose one day. "I suppose it will be years and years before we dance in a theatre, if we ever do."

"Oh, I don't know," said another girl, overhearing. "Some of us will dance in the Dominick at Christmas. Didn't you know that the school always gives a matinée just before Christmas? I was in it last year; just in the *corps de ballet*, of course. And then some of the younger ones do get occasional engagements."

"I didn't know that," said Drina. "I didn't think they'd let us. In pantomime, do you mean?"

"Well, sometimes. It's not exactly encouraged – in some ballet schools it's absolutely forbidden – but it has been known. There was a kid last year who was in a West End play for three months. She was really poor and needed the money, so they let her understudy. But she wasn't doing that for long, because the other girl got ill and she took over. It was Marlene Bellino in the next class."

"Oh!" cried Drina and Rose. They knew Marlene by sight: a lovely dark girl of thirteen, who was reputed to show great promise.

"But it won't happen to *us*," said Rose humbly.

The friendship with Rose prospered, and Mrs Chester freely admitted that she was a nice child, with excellent manners. And Drina found the little house at Earl's Court a great change from the always tidy and impeccably run flat. Rose's family were poor but, on the whole, cheerful, and her father was patently bursting with pride over his daughter.

"We'll see her on television yet," he said once, and Rose cried indignantly:

"Well, I'd like to think you will, in a way, Dad. But it will have to be because the Company is appearing. I want to be a real classical dancer, not just a television artist."

And her parents, who privately thought that to appear to millions of viewers at once was greatly to be preferred to performing in a draughty theatre to a few hundred, smiled indulgently.

So the term wore to an end, with Drina occasionally in high spirits but more often in a slight state of tension. They had the usual medical examination and nothing was said about her health, but Mrs Chester, knowing very well that her granddaughter's spirits were not very high, had planned that they should all go for a holiday to Switzerland for at least three weeks, and longer if possible.

"It will be lovely," said Drina. "But I shall miss the Dominick. Six weeks' holiday – think of it! And then we go back just for ballet lessons."

"Well, first you shall have a healthy time in the Alps," Mrs Chester said grimly.

Jenny was only going to the farm for a week or two; then she was off to Llandudno with her family, a fact that she was inclined to deplore. To Jenny, the height of bliss was to be caught up in the life of the farm, and she was not at all sure how she would like the North Wales resort, though she admitted in a letter to Drina that it would be nice to be by the sea.

Drina had been invited to go to Llandudno for part or the whole of the time, but as the Pilgrims would be there just at the time when the Swiss holiday was taking place it was impossible. Drina was sad to think that she would not see Jenny, but Mrs Chester promised that she should come for half-term at the end of October, if not before.

"But that's years away!" said Drina, looking at the summer trees as they walked through the park.

"It will come," said her grandmother.

Breaking up day arrived at the Dominick and they had their last ballet lesson of the summer. When they assembled again it would be September and already there might be a tang of autumn in the air. When Drina thought of that, Jenny's visit did not seem so far away.

She felt unaccountably dismal on that last day. There was really no reason for it, but she could have hidden herself in one of the cloakrooms and howled. Six whole weeks in which she could not practise properly; six whole weeks when she would hear no ballet talk.

But she did not dare to confess her feelings to her grandmother, as she knew that Mrs Chester would not sympathise. And actually, it was suddenly quite thrilling to think of crossing the Channel for the first time and seeing France and Switzerland and the snow-clad Alps. It would be a tremendous experience and, after all, they had recently been told in a lecture that the more experiences a dancer had the more she could put into her dancing.

Queenie was going to Belgium and Daphne to Ireland, but Rose was not going away at all. Drina felt rather guilty about that and wished that her friend could go with them to Switzerland, but she knew that it wasn't possible. It would cost too much for the Conways to agree.

Several of the foreign girls – most of them in upper classes – were going home, and the cloakrooms resounded on that last day with their excited voices.

The Chesters and Drina set off for Switzerland on August 7th, and Drina insisted on taking her ballet shoes with her, as she intended to practise if she could find anywhere suitable. The hotel they were going to was a big one and surely she would be able to find somewhere?

They crossed the Channel on a lovely calm afternoon and Drina enjoyed every moment of the journey, especially the strangeness of being tucked up in a sleeping-berth on the rocking French train.

She slept soundly and awoke to find that they were at the frontier and would soon be in Switzerland. But it was hours and hours before she caught her first glimpse of the snowy peaks of the Bernese Oberland and lunchtime before they left the train in a high mountain valley, where the sun shone brilliantly, a grey-green river rushed down from the glacier, and the mountains took her breath away.

The chalets and hotels all had colourful shutters and windowboxes, a Swiss band was playing, and people of many nationalities wandered up and down the long village street.

Drina's room had a tiny balcony, from which she could see the snowfields and glaciers, and as she stood there she felt quite unlike herself. It seemed really astonishing that Drina Adams should be in the high Alps, far from London and the Dominick School. There was a great tunnel through the mountains through which the electric trains sped towards Italy. Italy! Her father's country, and the country from which she had got her black hair and dark eyes and perhaps a little of her dancer's temperament.

For almost the first time, she felt real curiosity about Italy. After all, if she was half-Italian she ought to see her other country one day!

"Shall we ever go?" she asked, as they sat down to lunch in the charming dining-room.

"Not this time," said her grandmother firmly. "The Italian frontier could be reached in an hour or two, but we've done enough travelling. We'll have a real holiday, walking in the meadows and perhaps hiring a car and driving a little. But some day – perhaps next year – you shall go. I didn't think you felt any curiosity about Italy."

"I never did before, but our train was going on to Rome," Drina explained, "And suddenly I remembered about my father coming from Milan."

"Well, we'll take you next year almost certainly," her grandfather promised.

The proprietor and his wife were kindly people and very interested in the black-haired little English girl who was training to be a dancer. Frau Braun readily offered Drina an empty room where she could practise and Drina managed to put in an hour every morning, before going out to explore the village and to wander in the lovely, flowery meadows by the wild river.

The mountains were a never-ending source of wonder and joy to her, for she had never in her life seen anything so beautiful as the sunlight on that high ice and snow. She was rapturously happy and sent vivid flower postcards to Jenny, and Rose, and other friends at the Dominick, not forgetting Adele Whiteway, who was herself in Holland, but who had given Drina her address.

Drina grew very brown and strong and was soon able to walk long distances. She made friends with another English family, and several times went out for the day with the two girls and their brother. The

brother was nearly grown-up, so Mr and Mrs Chester made no objection to the excursions.

That way, Drina was able to explore some of the more remote mountain valleys, and one day they climbed right up to the foot of the glacier, where the grey ice curled up under the burning blue sky and the little river – a baby torrent – started off on its long rush down the green valley to the distant village and far beyond.

Drina wore a big scarlet straw hat and carried a little rucksack, and each evening she returned a shade more suntanned and eager to tell of all the wonders she had seen while her grandparents were having a quiet time in the valley.

Letters came from Jenny in Llandudno, and she seemed to be enjoying herself after all. She loved the sea, and they had been to Anglesey and once to Llanberis, from where they had climbed Snowdon to the very top.

"Of course it's not like the Alps," Jenny wrote. "But it was really thrilling. Oh, and we went to that little village under the headland where you stayed once – Porth-din-Lleyn – and I thought of you dancing on the headland, as you told me you did."

And Drina, on her Alpine balcony, looked back at that time that seemed so remote, when they had stayed at the cottage on the shore and she had fallen in love with the tiny Welsh village. She had meant to go back, and perhaps she would one day. Places, Drina was beginning to see, could be very fascinating. And she thought for the first time that if ever she realised her ambition and joined the Dominick Company she would almost certainly go abroad a good deal. Perhaps to Paris, and Milan, and Stockholm, and even Helsinki. The Company had gone to the far north of Europe only the previous autumn, so she had heard.

When they had been in Switzerland nearly a fortnight, they learned that there was going to be a concert in the hotel, and as many guests as possible were expected to perform. There would be a Swiss orchestra and the village yodelling club was going to be there.

Frau Braun said earnestly to Mrs Chester. "It would be nice if the little Drina would dance for us. We it would enjoy so much."

"Oh, I hardly think –" Mrs Chester began and then, seeing the disappointment on Frau Braun's face, wavered. "She has her shoes with her, of course, but what about the music? And then she hasn't anything suitable to wear."

Drina was rather overcome, for it was a long time since she had danced in public, but the more she thought about it the more she decided that she would like to dance in Switzerland. So she said. "I could wear my blue dress. It's very short and full. And there are a lot of records in the lounge."

"Well, run and see if there's anything suitable," said her grandmother.

So Drina quickly turned over the great pile of records and was lucky enough to find the music to which her Snow White dances had been made. So Frau Braun was delighted and Drina practised eagerly for the next few days.

When the night came, crowds of people arrived at the hotel for the concert, which was to be held in the huge dining-room after dinner. The meal was early so as to give time for the tables to be moved and the chairs arranged. People of many nationalities were there, and Drina began to feel a little nervous. What if she didn't dance well? What if she disgraced herself *and* her grandparents?

But in the end, she enjoyed every moment of it. The familiar music gave her confidence, and somehow the thought of the darkening Alps outside added an extra magic. She was four thousand feet high in the very heart of Switzerland!

She had tied her hair back with a blue ribbon and the blue dress was really quite a good dancing costume. Not like a tutu, of course, but then she had rarely danced in one lately, though they wore practice tutus occasionally at the Dominick School.

At the end of the dance there was a storm of applause, and Drina had to dance again. After the months of struggle and hard work, it was undoubtedly fun to dance before an uncritical audience and her happiness seemed to shine out as she moved lightly over the floor – so small, so dainty, looking much younger than nearly thirteen.

Afterwards, she sat by her grandmother and listened in a sort of enchantment to the lovely yodelling and the tuneful Swiss music.

It was late when she went up to bed, but she went out on to her balcony for a few minutes. The night was very still and starry and she could faintly see the shapes of the mountains. She could hear the river thundering down the valley and the melodious cowbells in the meadows.

"Lovely Switzerland!" she thought, and suddenly the future seemed entirely happy and full of hope. When she returned to the Dominick School, she would work hard again and perhaps she would be chosen to dance at the matinée in the Dominick Theatre.

Anything seemed possible at that moment and she wondered why she had ever been miserable. Life was really quite perfect.

# BOOK TWO
## A Future Ballerina?

# 1
# Autumn Term

**B**ack in London at the beginning of September, Drina felt in still higher spirits. In some ways, it was lovely to see the towers of Westminster again, to wake up to the sound of Big Ben and to be able to see the familiar Thames from her bedroom window, but she missed the Alps and the pretty village and she often looked back on that night when she danced as a particularly happy time.

When she first met Rose, her friend gave a startled shout.

"Oh, Drina, how brown you are! You look – why, positively Italian!"

"Well, I am, really," said Drina. "I told you my father was."

She herself felt sorry to see that Rose looked so pale and she was glad when her grandfather asked her friend to go into Bucks with them in the car on Saturday.

They went speeding westwards soon after breakfast and spent the day high on the hills, wandering in the beechwoods and looking out over the blue vale of Aylesbury. Because both girls were curious to see it, Mr Chester consulted a large-scale map until he found Chalk Green Manor, and they went by way of high lanes, overhung with trees, until they found the drive gates and the large board that said:

### CHALK GREEN MANOR
RESIDENTIAL BALLET SCHOOL
*For information apply to the Headmistress or to the Igor Dominick School, Red Lion Square, London, W.C.1.*

"How strange it must be for them!" marvelled Drina. "Shut away here in the beechwoods, with only that little village with the green and the flint cottages. But it's a beautiful place. I wish we could see more."

But of course it was still holiday time, and all the members of the residential school would still be scattered all over Europe and possibly even further afield.

"But they'll be back at the end of next week," said Drina.

It gave her great satisfaction to think of the students coming back to another term's work and, as they drove towards London, her mind was already busy, visualising the moment when she and Rose would run up the steps of the Dominick School again.

It was good to get her possessions ready for the new term, and Drina herself ironed her scarlet blouses and carefully pressed her school skirt. On the day before she was due back at the Dominick for ballet lessons, her grandmother took her to a really good hairdresser and her smooth, shining hair was cut into a beautiful shape, so that it swung silkily round her brown face.

"You look like a gipsy!" said Mrs Chester, as she took her to have tea and cakes afterwards. "But certainly a very well-groomed one!"

That night, Jenny telephoned and she and Drina managed to get in a good deal of rapid conversation.

"And good luck for tomorrow!" Jenny cried, as she put the receiver down at last.

Drina went to bed cheerfully and by a quarter to nine the next morning was running across Red Lion Square towards the Dominick School. The building had been painted during the long holiday, but her mother's ballet shoes were still in the hall and there was still the same faintly stuffy smell.

Rose arrived almost on her heels and several of the members of their class were in the cloakroom. Daphne, after a month in County Mayo, was very suntanned, which looked odd but rather attractive with her fair hair, and she greeted Drina in an almost friendly way.

Queenie was there, full of her holiday in Belgium, but Jill really seemed to have had the most exciting holiday of their group. She had flown to Australia to spend some weeks with her family in Sydney. While in London, she lived with her aunt.

Queenie did not look best pleased to find herself well outshone by a friend.

But there were others who were still pale from staying in London: girls who had done little more in the way of holidaymaking than going to the seaside for a day.

"We've no money for holidays," said one bluntly. "It's hard enough to keep me here. If I don't get one of the scholarships I shall have to leave at the end of this year."

A momentary silence fell as the less fortunate ones thought of the tragedy of having to leave the Dominick. It was, of course, Queenie who spoke first.

"If I was in that position I expect they'd beg me to stay on. After all, I *am* –"

"Beryl Bertram's daughter!" someone said wickedly.

"Well, of course. That's what I mean."

"You're not so much better than anyone else, so shut up!" Jill said quite fiercely, which startled Queenie but did not really penetrate her self-satisfaction.

Drina found herself with a new ballet teacher, as the classes all got a different teacher at the beginning of the school year. The new teacher was a little thing, with a startlingly loud voice and a reputation for having a sharp tongue. But nevertheless she had a friendly enough twinkle as she surveyed her new class.

"Now, make no mistake. I know just what you've been doing and more or less what to expect from you. And don't worry if we don't get far this morning. We're all bound to be slightly out of practice after the holidays."

Drina enjoyed that first lesson and was happy to be back at work again. The hour passed all too quickly and then they were free. She and Rose fed the ducks in St James's Park before separating to go home for lunch, and in the afternoon Drina went along to practise at Miss Whiteway's flat. Miss Whiteway was at home and busy on some new designs, but she paused to listen to Drina's account of the changes at the Dominick.

"They've painted it. I suppose you knew? And I've got a new ballet teacher – Miss Martin. And some of the girls haven't come back. Two out of my class have gone to Chalk Green because their parents are going abroad. I should hate to be so far away from things! It would be like being an exile."

"And the Company's in Paris," said Adele Whiteway, smiling at her eager face. "So you won't see them about for a bit. They're going on to Brussels and Zurich."

"We haven't seen them about for months. They were on the provincial tour before we broke up for the holidays. Oh, Miss Whiteway, it was lovely to be back, and I'm going to work hard this term. Do you think –

do you think there's the slightest chance of my being chosen for the Christmas matinée at the Dominick? I would so love that, but they say that only a few from each class get chosen, and Chalk Green joins in as well."

"Well, you might," said Adele Whiteway. "But if you don't –"

"Then I'll have to bear it. But I do so long to dance in a real theatre. I want to smell it from the back, and see the dressing-rooms, and what the stage looks like when you're on it. Just for an afternoon we might imagine that we're the real Company."

"Well, if not this year almost certainly next."

"Say I wasn't still there?"

"Of course you will be. Everyone is quite pleased with you and you're getting on well enough. I heard that you're very good at character. Quite a personality!"

"But I want to be a classical dancer," said Drina positively.

"Well, time will tell. And now you'd better get on with your practising."

A few days later, the school went back full time and, while the September sun poured down most warmly, the Juniors and Seniors got back into their stride.

A good deal was heard about the Christmas matinée and there was much speculation as to who would be chosen. The main ballet was to be *The Golden Fawn*, with choreography by Igor Dominick and settings by Miss Whiteway, and there were to be one or two *divertissements* as well. The dances from *The Golden Fawn* were already being taught in the various classes.

Drina put her whole heart into her work, both dancing and ordinary classes, and she really felt that her dancing was getting better. Miss Martin praised her warmly on one or two occasions and she no longer felt that she was struggling against odds. Her health was good and she felt full of life and energy.

The Dominick School was entirely familiar, and she now knew nearly everyone by sight, though on the whole the classes kept very much to themselves and there was not much mixing. Lena Whiteway, however, was always friendly and seemed to regard Drina as her special protégée.

The weeks passed and it was October; the trees in the parks were russet and gold, with the leaves occasionally fluttering down when the wind rose. The barrows in the streets were loaded with bright red apples, dahlias and early chrysanthemums, and in the evenings a smoky blue mist lay over the city, dimming the near and far spires.

It was early in October that something happened that had a good deal of significance, though Drina had no idea of it at the time. Quite often, they had play readings in class and Drina always enjoyed reading a part. She had a good voice, clear and sweet, and a certain amount of dramatic sense.

One afternoon, they were reading *A Midsummer Night's Dream* and Drina was given the part of Puck, which pleased her enormously. She sat there eagerly as they started the second act, her smooth hair swinging forward, and when she received her cue she plunged with enjoyment into Puck's first long speech.

"The King doth keep his revels here tonight;
Take heed the Queen come not within his sight;
For Oberon is passing fell and wrath,
Because that she, as her attendant, hath
A lovely boy, stolen from an Indian king;
She never had so sweet a changeling:

And jealous Oberon would have the child
Knight of his train, to trace the forest wild;
But she perforce withholds the loved boy,
Crowns him with flowers and makes him all her
joy:
And now they never meet in grove or green,
By fountain clear or spangled starlight sheen,
But they do square, that all their elves, for fear,
Creep into acorn-cups and hide them there."

It was only as she finished the speech and looked up
that Drina realised that Igor Dominick had entered and
was standing beside the teacher. The girl reading the
Fairy, who had noticed him too, stumbled and
spluttered nervously, for it was unheard of for Mr
Dominick to wander into an ordinary class. But he
waved his hand and said casually, "Go on!" and the
Fairy struggled miserably through her speech. She had
quite good technique as a dancer, but was certainly not
cut out to use her voice.

Drina was rather shy, certainly, but Igor Dominick
had said go on, so he must have meant it. She took up
her next speech with spirit.

"Thou speak'st aright;
I am that merry wanderer of the night.
I jest to Oberon and make him smile,
When I a fat and bean-fed horse beguile,
Neighing in likeness of a silly foal –"

When she looked up again the door was just closing
and she thought no more about the little episode.
There was quite enough to think about without that,
including the fact that Daphne was quite obviously
taking up the old rivalry.

Daphne yearned, just as they all did, to be picked for the matinée, and she realised that Drina had greatly improved. It would be more than Miss Daniety could bear if Drina Adams was chosen and she was not.

"I mind, too," Drina confided to Rose. "I mind awfully. But I shouldn't hate *her* if she was chosen. One of the things I don't like about this life is the awful rivalry."

"Well, it's bound to happen, I suppose," Rose said wisely. "We'll find it all the time, even if we do get into the Company one day. More if we do, perhaps. There's sure to be someone who wants to smack your face because you get a chance and she doesn't."

"Only we must try not to get like it ourselves," said Drina with a faint sigh. "We *must!*"

"*You* never will," Rose assured her, for she felt that Drina had great depth of character as well as a generous nature. "Daphne's not very nice, but Queenie is worse. I don't believe the most saintly person in the world could really like Queenie."

"Sometimes I don't feel a very saintly person when I'm with her," Drina admitted. "But I hate being at loggerheads with anyone."

# 2

# Disappointment for Drina

There were rumours throughout October that any day now the dancers would be chosen for *The Golden Fawn*, though the more experienced ones said that it would most likely be November.

November came and Marianne Volonaise, that glamorous and almost legendary figure, was suddenly seen no more about the building. It was said that she had flu and that the choice for the Dominick matinée would not be made until she was better. Meanwhile the dances continued to be practised in the many classes and the big building echoed to the simple but fascinating music. Nearly everyone was whistling and humming it and whenever Drina heard those airs in the future she remembered that wet late autumn and the anxious excitement that filled her heart as she went about her daily life.

Then Miss Martin gave them a lecture.

"I'm getting tired of all this tension. I wish we didn't give even the one show a year, for it upsets you all. Get it clearly in your minds that only a few from each class will be chosen and that it will not mean, if you're not chosen, that you're necessarily a bad dancer. It is far more likely to mean that, for some reason, you're not suitable for the roles available. Now, to the *barre*." And the music started again while they went through the familiar exercises.

But in the end, Marianne Volonaise was back and it was known that the choice would be made on the following Monday. In the rehearsal room, the members of the Company, long since back from their European tour, were rehearsing for the opening of the London season, which would take place soon after the New Year.

Drina had begged her grandfather to get seats for both the opening of the Royal Ballet at the Royal Opera House, Covent Garden, and for the later Dominick opening. She knew, with everyone else, that the Dominick Company was starting the season with three tried favourites, *Les Patineurs*, Act II of *Giselle*, and *Carnival*.

The Monday morning was soakingly wet, but everyone was at school early, keyed up for the important event to come. Drina, who knew that she had worked hard and had most definitely improved, alternated between hope and certain knowledge that she would not be chosen. And after all, she told herself fiercely, it didn't matter really. Learning to dance well was what mattered, practising so that her body would obey her easily and gracefully. Such ephemeral things as an afternoon backstage at the Dominick Theatre counted for only a moment in time and were not really important. But, all the same, her heart was beating high as they assembled in one of the studios.

The ballet classes had been staggered that day, so that Igor Dominick, Marianne Volonaise and the Company Ballet Mistress could be present at all of them in turn.

Drina took her place at the *barre* and began to warm up, thankful that the great ones were not yet present.

Just in front of her was Daphne, and behind her Rose whispered nervously:

"Oh, Drina, I feel awful! I *know* I won't be chosen, but Dad and Mum would be so thrilled if they could come and see me at the Dominick. I just haven't dared to say much about it at home, in case I'm not chosen."

"Granny just says not to worry," Drina remarked. "And I know she's right. But I should so love it."

When the class started properly there was still no sign of the three important people, but they entered quietly five minutes later and the whole class stopped work and curtsied.

"Carry on!" said Igor Dominick, and the three went and sat in the corner by the piano.

"Fancy them bothering about *us*!" Drina thought humbly. "We're so unimportant, really." But at the back of her mind was the further thought that, after all, some of them at least were the material that would be absorbed into the Ballet Company later; in four or five years, perhaps. A lifetime away!

Drina's mouth felt dry and her hands hot, but she tried hard to forget that anyone was watching. It was fairly easy at the *barre*, but not so easy during the centre practice, when she was looking straight into their corner. Marianne Volonaise was wearing an elegant coat loosely over her shoulders and looked paler and thinner than usual. She always looked to Drina rather like a princess, elegant and remote, though it was said that she was capable of fits of both temper and temperament.

Igor Dominick was watching intently, occasionally making a remark to the other two.

Drina cheered up when they began to do one or two of the dances from *The Golden Fawn*. She could never be miserable or tense when she was actually dancing;

the two just did not seem to go together. Daphne, with her fair hair held back tightly, was dancing with a will, and Queenie, near the front, was moving with her usual confidence.

Suddenly, though at first Drina didn't notice it, the secretary slipped in and joined the group in the corner. She had several slips of paper in her hand which she spread out on top of the piano.

Finally, they were told to stop and put on their cloaks, and at first Drina was scarcely conscious of what was happening. One by one, the girls whose names were called out went to stand a little apart. Queenie had gone, and Jill, and a pretty girl called Lorna. They were all to be Tree Fairies.

"Rose Conway!" Rose gave a little gasp as she heard that she was to be a Fawn.

"Daphne Daniety – also a Fawn." Daphne made a little sound, hastily stifled, that was almost a crow.

"Drina –" Miss Volonaise began in her beautiful voice, then stopped as Mr Dominick put out his hand and said something to her. "No, I'm sorry. That was a mistake. Meryl James, Bella Gionio –"

Drina stood frozen to the spot, clutching her familiar cloak round her. Miss Volonaise had been going to choose her and Mr Dominick had stopped her at the last minute. That could only mean that he thought her dancing bad, in spite of all that had been said about suitability.

She felt sick and her heart was pounding. The disappointment was bitter, especially as Queenie, Daphne and Rose had all been selected. Drina set her teeth and vowed that she would not let anyone know how much she minded, but to her dismay sharp tears stung her eyes.

"Don't be a baby, you idiot!" she admonished herself

fiercely, and stood staring straight ahead with fixed attention.

They were going. Mr Dominick was having a last word with Miss Martin. Someone ran forward to open the door and the great ones passed into the corridor. Miss Martin's voice, oddly far away, said:

"Class, dismiss, and please go straight off to the cloakroom. There's no need for discussion now." Then she put her hand on Drina's shoulder. "You run up to the office, will you, dear?"

"Me?" Drina gulped and brought her gaze back into focus.

"Yes."

"She's going to be chucked out!" said Queenie, quite audibly, and Jill hissed back.

"Shut up! You are a beast sometimes, Queenie!"

They all went off in a bunch, even the ones who had not been chosen, and Drina was left standing in the corridor. She felt rather as though life had suddenly come to an end.

"Go up to the office." Why? What had she done? She knew that she had improved after all her hard work. And yet she had not been chosen to dance in *The Golden Fawn*.

She trailed along dismally, with her cloak still held tightly round her. Up the stairs, along the upper corridor. The tears were much nearer the surface now, and she did not know how she was to keep them back. Halfway along the corridor she stopped and squeezed herself into a sort of alcove which had a curtain drawn over it. It was actually a sort of extra store cupboard, filled with records in cases, discarded ballet shoes, piles of music.

Drina crouched in there, fighting her tears, trying to find the courage to go along to the office to learn why she had been summoned. And while she crouched there she heard foosteps approaching and caught a glimpse, as she peered fearfully out, of the advancing figures of Igor Dominick and Marianne Volonaise. Miss Volonaise was saying:

"Are you sure it's wise? We never have encourgaed it."

"No, but we have allowed it to happen occasionally and on the whole it works – in certain cases. And I think this may be one of them. The child dances well for her age – good poise and technique – and though she seems shy she strikes me as having personality. There are times when she quite stands out in that little lot. Besides, I heard her reading Shakespeare myself – Puck – and she had a strong dramatic sense. And they want a really dark child who looks young."

Drina was so astonished that she forgot all about her tears. They were talking about *her*, she thought in amazement. Surely they must be? She was very dark and little, and she *had* read the part of Puck in front of Igor Dominick.

"But what about her dancing?"

"Oh, she can get in her usual class before rehearsals, and once the show goes on it will only be a matter of a matinée occasionally and being at the theatre until the beginning of the third act. It may not even mean a matinée. So many theatres now content themselves with two performances on a Saturday, the first at half-past five and the second following straight on. Campbell really is in a state and I told him I might consider helping him. He's applied to one or two of the stage schools and there's no one suitable. Most of them are already rehearsing for pantomime. He's completely sunk without a suitable child. Of course we'd have to ask her parents. How old is she?"

"Oh, about thirteen. There'd be no difficulty about a licence. And I believe the guardians are actually her grandparents. Adele Whiteway brought her to the audition, if you remember. I think Drina's quite a protégée of hers."

Drina was suddenly appalled to realise that they must have stopped right outside her hiding-place and that she shouldn't be listening. It was terribly wrong of her, even though she hadn't the slightest idea what they were talking about. She jammed her fingers firmly into her ears, comforted to realise that they did not seem to be considering asking her to leave the Dominick, though something was obviously going to happen.

With her fingers in her ears, she did not hear Marianne Volonaise say:

"What if it runs for a year or two?"

"Oh, the kid they've got now will be back in the late spring and could probably take over again. I'll stress it that that should be the arrangement, if possible."

"And if it *doesn't* run? It doesn't sound a sure winner to me."

"Then we'll see the quality of the child. I believe she really cares about her dancing. She'll have had an experience and if she has character she can use it wisely."

They passed on towards the office, and Drina slowly unstuffed her ears, blew her nose and emerged from her hiding-place.

She went very slowly towards the office and knocked, and Igor Dominick's voice told her to enter.

# 3

# A Chance for Drina

There was no one in the office but Mr Dominick and Marianne Volonaise, and Drina felt extremely small, unimportant and shy. She was bewildered, too, and still rather shaky from her disappointment and fright.

They looked at her in silence for a moment and then Marianne Volonaise asked gently, "What have you been crying about?"

"N-Not really crying," said Drina.

"You were disappointed not to be chosen for *The Golden Fawn*?"

"Yes, I thought – I thought it was b-because I was bad."

Igor Dominick was blowing his nose, but he paused to say:

"Oh, cheer up, child! Nothing of the sort. We've got something else to put to you, that's all. You may prefer it to being a fawn or a tree fairy for one short afternoon. How would you like to act in a West End play?"

Drina gaped.

"A p-play? But I'm not an actress. I'm a dancer. I mean I – I hope to be one day."

He chuckled and Marianne Volonaise smiled.

"Well said, Drina Adams. But it's a dancing part. There's not very much to say and I should think you'd manage a few lines all right. You've got a good clear voice."

Drina was more staggered than she had ever been in her life. A West End play, in a real theatre! It was like a dream, utterly unbelievable. When she had expected to work for years and years without ever stepping out of the crowd.

"I – I don't really understand."

"Small blame to you," Igor Dominick said. "It's like this. A friend of mine, Calum Campbell, who is a well-known producer, is putting on a play in December. It's called *Argument in Paris* and is a translation from the French. It had quite a success in Paris, incidentally. I'll tell you briefly that it's about a very beautiful, overbearing woman, who is being played by Marla Lerieu" – Drina gasped, for she knew a little about the theatre now, as well as about ballet – "and this woman has always fought with her husband as to whether they shall live permanently in Paris or at their place in the country. In the play, this suddenly boils up into an issue. Madame Le Brun insists that she can bear no other life than that of the city, and her husband, who is very much in love with her, but is the sort of composer who needs absolute quiet and peace, has to choose between his wife and his work. Their children also have to choose between their father and mother. Both girls adore their father. The elder girl is seventeen or eighteen, and the younger one is only twelve, and this is where you come in. For the little one, Francoise, is training to be a ballet dancer, and so she must not only choose between her father and mother for the next few years, but there is her career to think of as well. She chooses Paris and dancing. That's a very brief resumé, and the play has quite a few dramatic situations, but you get the gist of it?"

"Yes," Drina murmured, staring up at him with bright eyes and burning cheeks.

"Well, the girl who is at present rehearsing the part of Francoise is being taken to Australia unexpectedly by her parents. They're going very suddenly and they won't

consider leaving her behind. She's only just thirteen.
They'll be away for four or five months, anyway, and the
child who was understudying has broken her leg. Not
badly, but she'll be laid up for some time. They think they
may be able to to find another understudy, but they want
to be sure that they've got someone really good to play
Francoise. Do you think you could do it?"

"I – I don't know," Drina faltered.

"Well, would you like to go along in the morning
and try?"

"Yes. Yes, I think I would. Would I have to dance
much?"

"A little in the second act, I believe, and then at a
party in the first scene of Act Three. They would be
quite simple dances, and you could do them very well.
What about your grandparents? Would they mind?"

"I – I don't know," Drina said again, thinking of her
grandmother.

"Well, one of us will telephone and put it to them,
and you can explain more fully yourself. If you
definitely decide to go you can tell us in the morning
and someone will take you over to the rehearsal. It's at
the Queen Elizabeth Theatre, only a few hundred yards
away."

"Yes, I – I know it."

"And you need not feel that it'll upset your dancing
too much. You could probably get your ballet class in
here every morning before going to the rehearsal, and
you can take school work with you, so that you can get
on when you're not needed. Someone will have to
accompany you each time and see that you're all right.
And when the play goes on they'll have to take you
and bring you home."

Drina escaped soon after that and went back to her
classroom with a wildly beating heart and cheeks still

burning fiercely. But when she got there it was just about time for break, and everyone crowded round her as she drank her milk.

"What is it, Drina? You look strange and excited. Are you to be in *The Golden Fawn* after all?"

"Oh, I do hope so!" Rose breathed at her side.

"No," Drina said, taking such a large gulp of milk that she nearly choked. "No. I'm to go and be tried for a real play." And she poured out what she had learned about *Argument in Paris*.

They were deeply interested and more than a little envious. It made *The Golden Fawn* fade away into insignificance to think of Drina Adams dancing in a West End theatre, not for one performance, but perhaps for months.

"Only of course you won't get the part," said Queenie, with a toss of her head.

When they went back into class, Drina did her best to work, but her thoughts were whirling and, at twelve o'clock she could not get home quickly enough. Her grandmother met her at the door.

"Well, Drina! Mr Dominick himself has been on the telephone. What's all this rubbish about a West End play?"

"D-didn't he tell you?" Drina faltered.

"Well, he did, and very clearly and concisely. It seems he doesn't think it would harm your dancing, and he even said it would help to bring out your personality. I said I'd think about it and let him know later. And I got your grandfather on the telephone and asked him what he thought."

"Oh!" said Drina anxiously.

"He said he leaves it to me. And I'm sure I don't know if it would be right to agree."

Drina washed her hands and sat down at the lunch

table. She forced herself to swallow her soup, because the thing that was sure to upset her grandmother still further would be if she didn't eat well.

"Oh, Granny, I think I would like to try. But, of course, Mr Campbell may not think me good enough."

Mrs Chester surveyed the flushed, anxious face thoughtfully. Igor Dominick had said a good deal, in his brisk way, and she had no intention of repeating most of it. He had talked of what Drina's dancing teachers said. That she showed some talent and had no fear of hard work, but that she obviously lacked confidence. Everyone thought that it could not harm her to take the part if it was offered.

"But it would mean organising things," Mrs Chester said aloud, with a sigh. "Just as I had to with Betsy. Once or twice she took professional roles when she was still only a child. I know what I shall do if you get the part. I shall get in touch with someone I used to know very well. I believe she still lives in London and there's just a chance that she may be free. She has taken various jobs as chaperone to stage children, and she is a well educated woman, though growing elderly now, I suppose. If she agreed she could take you to the theatre, and –"

"But I *know* my way to the theatre!" Drina protested.

"Of course you do, but surely you know that you'll have to have someone to look after you and see that you do your school work? Dear me! We'll have all the bother of getting you a licence and so on."

"Would you mind so terribly, Granny?" Drina asked guiltily.

"Yes, in a way. You know very well that it isn't what I want for you. But you know your own mind as well, and if this is what *you* want I suppose you must have your chance. But I hope it won't unsettle you. It would some children."

"It won't," Drina promised. "I'll still work hard at my dancing, and – and when it's over I'll be just a Junior at the Dominick again."

"Plays don't always run for long, even in the West End. You realise that?"

"Yes, Granny." But Drina could not imagine the play ending when it had not even begun.

"Oh, very well, then. I can see you're determined, so I suppose I shall have to agree. I'll telephone the Dominick this afternoon."

"What shall I wear when I go to the theatre?"

"I should think your practice clothes, but you'd better take a tutu in case it's more an audition than a rehearsal."

Drina went back to the Dominick in a whirl of excitement, but forced herself to work hard that afternoon. It would never do if they stopped her going to the Queen Elizabeth Theatre in the morning because she was neglecting her school work.

The secretary found her as she was leaving after school.

"Drina, it's all arranged. You're to go over to the Queen Elizabeth in the morning at half-past ten, and someone from here will take you. If you get the part your grandparents must make some arrangement for an escort in the future. Take both practice clothes and a tutu."

That night, Drina telephoned Jenny and told her the exciting news, and Jenny was immediately wildly thrilled.

"Oh, Drina, will it be on at Christmas? Shall I be able to see you?"

"You're coming to stay after Christmas, so I expect

you can," said Drina. "It opens on December 8th. Oh, Jenny, isn't it miraculous? But I haven't got the part yet."

"You will take Hansl with you!" said Jenny.

"I always do, but he can't make Mr Campbell like me if I'm not good."

"Idiot! You will be good. Won't Daphne envy you?"

"She hates me," said Drina dismally. "She's in *The Golden Fawn*, but she doesn't care about that now. She thinks it should have been her, and Queenie thinks it should have been *her*. But it has to be someone little and dark, and Queenie isn't little. Besides, she's got a funny voice, and she doesn't read plays well."

"Anyway, good luck!"

Drina went to bed in a state of nervous excitement. But she read one of her favourite books for half an hour, then, soothed, turned out the light and almost immediately fell asleep.

# 4

# Dancing Part

The morning was cold and grey, but Drina felt warm with excitement. She was so thoroughly glad that she was not to be thrown out of the Dominick, but was to be given a special chance instead, that she hardly had room for being afraid. It mattered immeasurably to her that Igor Dominick and Miss Volonaise, in the midst of all their important work, had both picked her out and given her their attention. The dark man who held all their destinies in his hands believed in her, at least to the extent of thinking that she could dance on a real stage, and everything else paled before that. The nightmare time after yesterday's ballet class was already fading.

She took her place at the *barre* as usual and worked with a will, but straight afterwards, instead of going to the history class, she had to get ready to go to the theatre. Miss Martin herself was taking her, it appeared, and Drina was glad.

"What shall I have to do?" she asked, suddenly scared, as they stepped out into Red Lion Square.

"Watch the rehearsal first, I believe. It's rather an unusual case, of course. The girl who was originally given the part is still playing it. She doesn't leave till Saturday.

They walked briskly, Drina swinging her little case. As they approached the Queen Elizabeth Theatre she found that she felt shaky and odd. After all, it was quite a new experience, and all her innate doubts came flooding back. What if, by lunch time, she knew that she was not good enough?

Miss Martin marched her past the front entrance of the theatre, where the posters announced that the present show was called *South Sea Love Affair*, and into a narrow side street to the stage door. She gave Drina's name to the doorkeeper and then they were in a maze of dimly lighted, coldly stuffy passages, with draughts whistling from under doors.

Drina felt small and scared, and one side of her would have liked to turn tail and run back to the safety of the Dominick School. But the other side – the side that had dancing and the theatre born in her – thrilled to the very smell and atmosphere of the place. There were voices in the distance and suddenly they were through a door and in the wings.

For the first few minutes, Drina was completely bewildered. She dimly realised that the beautiful woman in red trousers and a black sweater must be the famous actress Marla Lerieu, and that the slim, dark little girl in practice costume must be Angela Blackmore, whose part she might be taking over. Various other people were sitting about on the stage, and a tall, fair man in a very bulky anorak was talking to two women who were also in outdoor clothes. But he came over to Miss Martin and Drina and greeted them warmly.

"We're just starting. Best thing the kid can do is to watch from the front and see what we want. Then she can read through the part and let us see her dancing. She *looks* just right, anyway." And he stared

appraisingly at Drina. "Almost *looks* French."

"I believe she has Italian blood," remarked Miss Martin.

"Well, here's the book and we'll get on. We've wasted enough time."

Drina thought in a panic that *they* had wasted his time somehow, though it was still barely half-past ten, but Miss Martin whispered reassuringly in her ear that rehearsals never did start on time and always went on until long after people were dropping with fatigue.

It was a fascinating experience for Drina, and she almost forgot that her ordeal was still to come. It was so odd to be in the stalls, with the big theatre stretching away behind her, dark and empty. It was strange to see the stage in the harsh electric light and the actors and actresses looking chilly and unglamorous. The pretty girl who was playing the elder daughter, Cecile, was yawning and shivering, and it certainly seemed to be very cold. Oddest of all, perhaps, was the fact that the French play was going to be acted in front of a set that depicted, evidently, the vividly blue sea and palm treas of the current South Sea island play.

"We'll take Act Two," said Calum Campbell. "We spent all our time on the first act yesterday, and, anyway, it'll give the kid a chance to see."

The whole play seemed to take place in the Le Bruns' Paris flat and Drina was soon absorbed, fascinated by the way the characters seemed real, even though they wore jeans and polo-necked sweaters. She watched with great intentness as Cecile went through the scene with her young lover, an artist from Montmartre, when he implored her not to go and bury herself in the country with her father. And she sat bolt upright when Angela made her entrance. The copy of the play that she held said, "Enter Francoise from the left, wearing ballet tights and a leotard. She had just been practising and is still a little lost in her own secret world."

Angela, that is Francoise, was startled into awareness when she learned of the argument that was in progress; at first unbelieving and then frantic.

"But we can't never see Father! Why won't he stay here, too? I can't *bear* it if he goes back to the country by himself!"

"He won't be alone. I'm going with him," Cecile explained. "At least, I'm almost sure. He's got to have someone there who cares, or he'll never finish his symphony. You know he can't work here. He's tried and it's hopeless. Besides, I don't think that he and Mother are very happy any more."

Drina's eyes pricked with tears as she watched Francoise realising that she must choose between her dancing career and her beloved father.

"But even if he goes now to write his symphony, *surely* he'll come back?"

"I don't know. He hates Paris. He hates this life that Mother leads; all parties and smart, noisy people. I'm torn, too. I don't want to leave Jacques. But I think I shall go. I suppose *you'll* choose your dancing?"

Francoise looked little and lost.

"It seems to be the only thing you care about."

"It's not! I care about Father, too. I want him to be here. He always makes me feel so safe. A – A sort of gentle rock."

"But when you're dancing you don't even think about that."

Francoise burst into tears.

"I *must* dance! I can't give it up! At least, I don't think I can. Madame said yesterday that some day I m-might be good. How *can* I go away from Paris?"

"Well, you'll have to choose. Father or ballet. Poor

kid! It is hard. Why isn't Mother different?"

"She's beautiful and everyone loves her."

"But hard. She doesn't care at all about Father's music. I wish, wish, wish we were an ordinary family and that we could be happy!" And Cecile made her exit.

Left alone, Francoise walked slowly and droopingly up and down and then began slowly to do a few ballet movements. Then she crumpled up on the stage and sobbed.

"Oh, why do I have to choose?"

"All right, Act Three, Scene One," said Calum Campbell, from the front. "Some of that was pretty grim, but we'll let it go now. Party scene. Everyone ready?"

Drina's heart was with Francoise. How terrible for anyone to have to choose between dancing and going to live in the country with a beloved father! She remembered her own bitter misery when she had thought she would never be allowed to dance again and easily created in her mind, in spite of the blue sea and palms in front of her, the luxurious flat, with busy, bustling Paris outside. She imagined the little Francoise hurrying away to her ballet school, dancing in some bare studio and thinking of her difficult home life. Poor Francoise!

The first part of the next scene bored her rather, for it was very grown-up and sophisticated, but she stiffened again when Francoise was called to dance for the guests. Francoise was still miserable and tense, and she danced badly at first. But gradually she seemed to forget herself and danced with enjoyment. Then suddenly she stopped and cried:

"I can't! I can't give it up! I'll have to stay in Paris!"

There could be no other decision, Drina knew, but

how little comfort Francoise would get from her shallow, flirtatious, unfeeling mother.

It was quite a shock when the scene ended and Drina was called up on to the stage. A book was thrust into her hands and she was told to read the part.

Back they went to the second act, and Drina at first felt quite breathless. Why, oh why had she ever thought she could act with a real Company? But Marla Lerieu gave her a warm smile and said, "Don't worry, dear! You'll do it all right." And she stood there, clutching the book tightly, telling herself that she was Francoise and not Drina Adams at all.

After a few moments she read clearly and well, and when Cecile had made her exit she dropped the book and did a few ballet steps, sadly, slowly. She had quite forgotten the watching people as she tumbled down in a tearful heap as Angela had done. She was Francoise in Paris, breaking her heart because she had to choose.

One or two people clapped, and Calum Campbell came on stage and slapped her so hard on the back that she staggered.

"Not bad at all! There was quite a lot of feeling in that. OK. We'll have a short break and you run off and put on a ballet dress, if you've brought one. And have you got some music?"

Miss Martin produced the music and Drina was led off to a small, shabby dressing-room where she changed hastily. It was very cold in the dressing-room, but she hardly had time to think about it. When she went back into the wings, the party scene was well under way, and someone pushed her forward for her entrance, once more thrusting the book into her hands.

Only the play mattered and Drina read Francoise's few words quite unselfconsciously; then, as the piano struck up, she began to dance. It had been decided that she might as well do one of the dances from *The Golden Fawn* that she had been practising, though of course she would have to do another one for the actual performance. It was a strange feeling at first to be dancing on that big stage, under the glaring lights, but then once again she was Francoise, dancing to her mother's friends and thinking about her choice. Without any help from the book, she stopped abruptly and cried so clearly that her voice rang to the very back of the gallery:

"I can't! I can't give it up! I'll have to stay in Paris!"

"You were really good," said Angela Blackmore, following her to the dressing-room. "You're sure to get the part. Mr Campbell has been simply frantic."

"Oh, do you really think so? Don't you mind dreadfully, though?" Drina asked.

Angela's hair was black and curly and she ran her hand through it.

"Terribly. I adore being Francoise. But I've got to go to Australia. My parents don't really like me acting. They made me refuse a film contract in the summer, but then they said I could take this. Only then my father found he had to go to Sydney. I don't want to go at all. I only want to act. Have you done anything before? You look terribly young!"

"I was thirteen last month. No, nothing else, except dancing occasionally at shows and in the school play. I'm at the Dominick School."

"That's just ballet, isn't it? Not a stage school?"

"Yes. I want to be a classical dancer."

Drina said no more, for she had found her first taste of the straight theatre very fascinating. But she knew in her heart that acting would never take the place of ballet.

When she and Angela went back, Mr Campbell was

talking to Miss Martin.

"I'll ring up the Dominick, then. Has the child got an agent? Oh, well, we'll see about it. Can she turn up in the morning? All right, then. And tell Dominick I'm grateful. The kid *looks* the part, and I believe she'll put her heart into it."

Drina was borne off then.

"Am I to be Francoise? Have I got it?"

Miss Martin looked at her with a friendly smile.

"You have. But don't let it make you slack at your dancing, my child."

"I won't. I promise. I only care about dancing."

"That's how it should be. But you certainly know how to speak. Was your mother an actress?"

"No," said Drina, with perfect truth. "No. But I liked it this morning."

It was so late that she went straight home, and over lunch she poured out her new experiences to her grandmother.

# 5

# First Night

After that, life was very full for Drina. Everything happened so quickly, too. She met Miss Thorne, a pleasant-faced elderly lady, who was to take her to the theatre and help her with her school work; the contract was signed and application made for a licence.

Miss Thorne, of course, knew that Drina's mother had been Elizabeth Ivory, but she was sworn to secrecy and Drina knew that she would never tell a soul. She liked Miss Thorne from the first moment and was to find her a very sensible person when things were worrying or troublesome. She also found Miss Thorne's stories of theatrical children extremely fascinating, but best of all, of course, was the fact that she could talk about her mother. Drina was still hungry to know more about red-haired Betsy and she was soon able to add several pleasing tales to her growing store of knowledge. Sometimes the child that her mother had been was so real that she could scarcely believe she had never seen her herself.

Drina's life settled down into ballet lessons at the Dominick, and then rehearsals interspersed with school work. If the rehearsal was over early, or she was not required any more, she went back to the Dominick School and took her place in class.

Some of the others were very busy with rehearsals for *The Golden Fawn*, but they were interested in Drina's experiences and very envious, too. But Daphne and Queenie stayed aloof. Queenie was furious that Beryl Bertram's daughter had been passed over and Daphne was remembering how Drina had had better parts than she at the Selswick School.

"Of course she'll get horribly stuck up now she's going to be in a real play!" Queenie said nastily to the cloakroom at large.

"Well, she won't, then!" Rose said fiercely, for she had never forgotten how Drina had championed her over the shabby coat and she was no longer afraid of Queenie and her airs. "Drina is nice. Really natural and kind. Only of course *you* wouldn't understand that. She'll never be spoilt and silly."

"Talk about hero worship!" said Queenie, and turned away.

Some of the older girls congratulated Drina and Lena Whiteway was delighted. So was Adele Whiteway when she heard all about it.

"I'm very glad, Drina. It's a real chance, so long as you don't let it spoil you. And I'm sure you won't. I must come to the opening night."

"Granny and Grandfather are coming, too, of course," said Drina eagerly. "I'll get tickets for you all. Lovely seats near the front!"

The rehearsals were sometimes unnerving, for Mr Campbell had a noisy temper at times, but more often fascinating. Drina learned her part very quickly and the dance she was to do at the party had been settled. Angela had gone off to Australia, with a load of presents from the cast, and Drina had one short note from her.

"I often think of you on that dirty, draughty old

stage. You don't know how lucky you are. But I hear it's bitterly cold in London and here the sun's shining. Good luck!"

It *was* cold in London, and Mrs Chester insisted that Drina must wrap up well. But she kept very healthy and had lost some of her doubts and tension. Her dancing seemed to be progressing well, and everyone seemed to be satisfied.

Once, she came face to face with Igor Dominick on the steps and he grinned at her.

"Everything going well? You seem to be thriving on it, anyway! When do you open?"

"On the 8th, Mr Dominick," said Drina.

"Well, don't expect too much, my child. It's not a good play. It seems to have lost a lot in translation."

Drina, of course, was too close to *Argument in Paris* to be able to judge and, in any case, she had almost no experience of plays, good or otherwise. The play seemed to her highly dramatic in places, especially at the end when the curtain went down to Charles Le Brun's wild piano playing, but it was quite a long time before she saw the play straight through and fully sorted out the story.

She grew very excited as the first days of December passed and the 8th loomed ahead. Her costumes, of course, were quite simple. In the second act she was to wear her ordinary practice clothes, and in the third, for the party, a lovely crisp pink ballet dress, with her hair tied back with matching pink ribbon.

Her grandmother took her to have her photograph taken in the pink dress and it was to hang in the theatre entrance with the others. Once or twice, Drina thought wistfully that it would have been wonderful if her name could have been in the programme as Andrina Adamo, but she had made her vow and it certainly was not the time to alter it. Andrina Adamo was for when she had really proved herself and would not disgrace Elizabeth Ivory. Of course she had sometimes been called that at the Selswick, but Daphne had either forgotten or was not interested.

So there was her name in the programme – "Francoise Le Brun played by Drina Adams". And then in a footnote: "Drina Adams appears by permission of the Igor Dominick Ballet School."

As soon as the programmes were available, Drina sent one off to Jenny, and received a picture postcard of a grey kitten in reply, with scrawled on the back:

"What an honour to know you! I'm really thrilled! By the way, Esmeralda is very well and hopes to see you one day."

And Drina paused for a moment, staring at the kitten, wondering when she would see the farm again.

But though she was looking forward to the 8th, she had really very little idea of the difference it would make to her life. She had settled down into the routine of rehearsals and the odd hours at the Dominick School, and in one way it seemed as though things could go on like that for ever.

Life was even fuller than it had been when she first went to the Dominick School and the atmosphere of the theatre hung over her always. She loved everything about it: the shrouded auditorium, the dark and cold passages behind the scenes, the endless, interesting talk of the others. The rest of the cast tended to make a pet of her and she found their stories of past triumphs and failures wonderfully fascinating. From them, she really began to get some idea of the glories and bitter disappointments of life in the theatre. She learned about the horrors of "resting", when it seemed that another suitable job might never be found, about touring in the provinces, and of the strange vagaries of fate that made some plays run comfortably to full houses for years and others, possibly equally good, that folded up in a few weeks. She heard of arrant failures, when the theatre doors were closed after three or four days, of the differences of film and television work.

The girl who played Cecile was only seventeen, but she had been working in the theatre since she was twelve and she assured Drina that she had played in most of the bigger provincial theatres.

"Oh, some of it's horrible, of course. Bad digs, and rotten bad-tempered landladies, and Sunday travel, and things going wrong – like costumes and scenery being delayed. But I wouldn't have any other life. This is my first real West End chance. If only it runs I can settle down and enjoy myself for a while and feel safe."

Drina very much liked the girl who was under-studying the part of Francoise. She was just fourteen and her name was Bernadette Gray. She was small, pale and very dark and rather shabbily dressed, and she had been at a stage school for three years.

Privately Drina thought that it must be terrible to be an understudy with very little chance of ever appearing on the stage, but Bernadette didn't seem to mind. She said frankly that she was glad of the money and added that she had been ill and didn't seem to have much energy. It was a nice rest after pantomime. Last year, she had been in *Robinson Crusoe* in one of the outlying theatres.

"*That* was tiring, if you like. But mind you, Drina, I'm not typical. Most of my friends are bursting with ambition, but just now all I want is some peace."

"Well, I hope it isn't too dull for you," Drina said guiltily, hoping that Bernadette was telling the truth.

A great deal that she heard in the theatre Drina did not fully understand, but her outlook was broadening every day, and at least there was no possibility that she would look on life in the theatre as a rosy dream. She undoubtedly heard more about the sorrows than the joys. When she repeated some of it to Adele Whiteway, she smiled and said:

"You *are* learning at first hand! But things may be different for you. If you're taken into the Dominick Company after a few years you'll always be sure of work and you'll be spared the worst uncertainties. Though you'll see plenty of the provincial theatres and won't avoid trouble with digs and landladies."

"And I'll go abroad," said Drina, clasping her hands round her knees.

"That, too. But you're likely to see more of Liverpool, Manchester, Newcastle and Glasgow. Not the smaller places, probably, as the Dominick is too big a Company to be able to be accommodated on small stages. It needs a really big one like the Empire Theatre, Liverpool, or Manchester Opera House."

Drina had fully expected that anyone so important as Marla Lerieu would ignore her, but she never did. She was a kind, good-tempered woman, as well as a first rate actress, and she had a daughter of her own, of just about Drina's age, at a boarding-school in the country.

"Doesn't she want to act?" Drina once ventured, when they were drinking tea together during a lull in the rehearsal.

Marla shrugged.

"Yes, she does, but I want her to have a really healthy life, at least until she's fifteen. I've seen too much of the theatre to want to pitchfork her into it when she's only a child. She's heard about you, though, and seems to be getting very restive. Though

I've told her that you're a dancer and want to go in for pure classical ballet."

And Drina was quite startled to think that Marla Lerieu's daughter should be envying her from that peaceful country boarding-school.

"I *know* I'm one of the luckiest girls in the world!" she said to Rose, as they wandered along Shaftesbury Avenue towards Piccadilly Circus after school one Friday afternoon, stopping at every theatre to look at the photographs and posters.

*Argument in Paris* was to open on the following Monday and, as they did not see quite so much of each other as formerly, they sometimes walked a little after school, before separating. Rose to get the Tube to Earl's Court, and Drina to cut south to the flat in Westminster.

The South Sea island play had finished at the beginning of December, so the dress rehearsal was to be on the Saturday, so that everyone could have a rest before the opening night. Miss Thorne called for Drina and when they arrived at the theatre the stage looked very different, for the scenery for the play was in place and at last it had taken on the glittering modernity of the Paris flat. There was a huge window, showing some of the city rooftops and Sacre Coeur against the sky.

Drina had a dressing-room to herself, but Bernadette Gray was allowed to sit there, knitting to pass the time, or else getting on with her school work. During the rehearsals she had worked with Drina and Miss Thorne.

It was thrilling to be made up and the whole atmosphere was brisker and more urgent. Stage hands hurried up and down the passages, Mr Campbell had a fit of temper out on the stage before the curtain rose and, as Drina wandered up and down waiting for her call, she thought, not for the first time, that it was all like a dream. She, Drina Adams, back stage of the Queen Elizabeth Theatre, waiting to appear in a real play!

The dress rehearsal was rather an unnerving business and it went on for so long that she was very tired when at last she was free to go home. Mrs Chester insisted on a very early night and said that, as the weather had turned brighter, she had better get out when Rose came to tea the next day.

Rose arrived at half-past two on Sunday afternoon and they walked briskly along Millbank, went into the Tate Gallery to see a few of their favourite pictures, and then walked on towards Chelsea, enjoying the sharp air, the winter sunlight and the feeling of being free. They turned away from the river up Cheyne Row and lingered before many of the charming houses.

"I'd love to live here somewhere," said Rose, as they wandered up and down many a quiet little street. "In a dear little house with blue shutters and trees in blue tubs."

They walked back beside the river as dusk fell, a cold blue dusk that gave London a touch of magic. Drina always loved the city in the evening and never so much as when the river mists were faintly blue and the towers of Westminster looked like a backcloth for some wonderful ballet.

They had muffins and then played paper-games with Mr and Mrs Chester. At half-past seven, Mr Chester fetched the car and ran Rose home. Drina went, too, for she always loved speeding along the lighted roads.

"Tomorrow!" she thought, as they drove back, and her heart seemed to turn over. Tomorrow the curtain would go up before a real audience and the critical eyes of the London theatre-going public would be on her. It was a wonderful and terrifying thought.

"Soon be Christmas!" remarked her grandfather, as they returned along the deep length of Victoria Street. "An unusual Christmas for you, Drina. The theatre every night except Christmas Day."

Drina's one regret was that she would not be able to go to Covent Garden, after all. It would somehow have crowned the year of hard work and new experiences to stand in the great foyer again, in the midst of the glittering first night crowd, remembering the Drina Adams who had stood there a year before, clutching a coffee cup in her unsteady hand and savouring the incredible news that her mother had been Ivory.

But the play, of course, came first. The play was a miracle that she could never have imagined a year before.

At first, Monday seemed quite an ordinary day; more ordinary, in fact, than any day for some time. She was not required to go to the theatre, so, after her ballet lessons, she went with the others into class and did history, English and French. End of term exams would soon be upon them and she was very anxious to do well, so that no one could say she had neglected her school work while rehearsing for *Argument in Paris*.

"Aren't you *scared*, Drina?" Rose asked, during break that afternoon, and Drina nodded.

"Horribly! My stomach feels all squirmy and I keep on imagining that something terrible will happen, like my ballet shoe coming undone, or missing an entrance."

"But don't they say 'Overture and beginners, please!' And then 'Your call, Miss Adams!'? I don't believe you *can* miss an entrance. Oh, Drina, I do envy you!"

But, as she ate a peaceful tea with her grandmother, Drina suddenly did not envy herself. She was most definitely a prey to first night nerves, and Mrs Chester looked uneasily at her pale face and tense attitude.

"Perhaps," thought Drina. "Miss Thorne will be late. Perhaps the taxi will get held up in a traffic jam. Perhaps I shall be sick and Bernadette will have to do it."

Her grandparents were to drive to the theatre in time for the rise of the curtain at 7.30, but Drina had to be there earlier.

Before she left the flat, a number of people had telephoned to wish her good luck and when she reached the theatre – quite safely, in spite of her fears – she was amazed to see a great pile of letters and cards. There was even a cable from Angela Blackmore, saying: "Thinking of you, Drina. Good luck."

How nice of Angela to be thinking of her from the other side of the world!

When she was ready in her practice clothes, and with her make-up on, Drina fished in her case and brought out Hansl. She put him on her dressing-table and looked at him for a long moment. It was nearly twelve years since that night when Hansl had been left in Elizabeth Ivory's dressing-room at the Dominick Theatre.

"Mother didn't know that he would be with me for my very first night," Drina thought, and the sight of the little black cat was strangely comforting.

Waiting was a strange time. She knew that the curtain had gone up and that the first act was passing. Once she wandered into the wings and stood there, feeling cold and strange, in a dream world, imagining that she really *was* Francoise, already dimly conscious that something was wrong between her father and mother. Francoise practising alone at the *barre*, before that sad little scene with Cecile.

During Scene One of the second act she limbered up, finding her nerves calmed by the familiar exercises. Again she was Francoise, a young girl in Paris, driven by the desire to dance and a prey to vague anxiety.

And when the time came for her entrance she was no longer afraid, no longer thinking at all about that critical first night audience. The play might be good or bad, but it was entirely real to Drina.

In the second interval, she changed into her pink ballet dress and the dresser helped her to tie the broad pink ribbon round her hair. She had pink ballet shoes, too. She thought that she looked unlike herself in her make-up, and she sat there, not talking to anyone, even Bernadette, still half Francoise.

The third act started. The guests were arriving. At last her call came and she stood in the wings, waiting for her cue. It came and she made her entrance into the blaze of lights, shrinking a little, half-proud. Wanting to dance, but conscious all the time of all that lay behind the brittle gaiety, of the choice she must make. Her "father" went to the piano; the music of her dance began.

She was still Francoise for quite a while after she had made her final exit, and with Francoise's sadness.

That first night she was to wait till the end, and by the time the curtain came down she was herself again, Drina Adams, and in a way happier and more alive than she had ever been. Her grandparents came behind to take her home. There were flowers for her, and a big box of chocolates, with a note that said, "From Jan. You were really good."

London was glittering with lights and it was snowing a little.

"You were very good," said her grandfather warmly, as he swung the car into Whitehall. "But it didn't strike me as being a good play. Still, we'll see what the critics say in the morning."

Drina was by then so sleepy that she scarcely realised what he meant.

# 6

# New Year's Eve

**D**rina slept well and awoke feeling refreshed and ready for anything. She dressed in her school clothes and went to help her grandmother to get the breakfast, but was arrested by the sight of a huge pile of newspapers on the table in the little hall.

"Goodness! What are they all for?"

"For you. But you'll never have time to look at them now," said her grandfather, appearing ready for the office.

"Oh!" cried Drina. In theory she knew quite well that, after a first night, critics wrote about the play in the newspapers, but it was hard to believe that it would happen to *Argument in Paris*. For the first time, she thought in fright that it would be awful if the London critics hadn't liked it, and yet surely they must when Marla Lerieu was so famous an actress?

"You really won't have time to look at them all before school," said Mr Chester.

"I suppose she'll be able to manage some," said her grandmother resignedly. "The coffee isn't ready yet. No, don't help me, Drina. You look at the papers. You've got to get it over, I suppose, but don't be too miserable if it gets bad notices."

The first one that Drina unearthed was brief and to

the point. The critic referred caustically to "this melodramatic and pointless little piece" and said that even Marla Lerieu's first-class acting could not save it.

"Oh!" cried Drina again. "The beast! Everyone worked so hard, and –"

Her grandfather looked over her shoulder.

"Oh, well, he's one of the most stringent critics writing today. It takes a masterpiece, perfectly performed, to please him. But you haven't read on."

Drina read on, with wide eyes and parted lips.

"The part of the young Francoise was charmingly played by thirteen-year-old Drina Adams. She obviously lacks experience, but she was completely at home in the wistful part of the French child who has to choose between the dancing to which she is already dedicated and her beloved father. As we are told that Drina Adams appears by permission of the Igor Dominick Ballet School this is perhaps not surprising."

"Well, that's high praise," said Mr Chester with satisfaction.

"She'll be getting her head turned," said Mrs Chester, coming in with the toast.

"Not she. Drina isn't the kind. A few words of praise never hurt anyone, unless they're completely above themselves already."

"What does the *Daily Mail* say?" cried Drina, feverishly struggling with the sheets.

The critic was brief and not over-enthusiastic.

"*Argument in Paris* immediately strikes one as having suffered a good deal in translation. It has some good situations, but on the whole is over-dramatised. Marla Lerieu does her best as the selfish, pleasure-loving wife and, as usual, she charms us with her soignée appearance and restraint, but the play lacks point and the third act inevitably leaves us with the uncomfortable thought that none of it was worthwhile. Lally Devine gives a pleasant performance as the elder daughter, Cecile, and James Barr-Ryan is occasionally moving as the composer who must have peace for his work."

By the time the breakfast was ready, the room was littered with newspapers and Mrs Chester's lips were pinched slightly. She liked early mornings to be quiet and well-ordered.

"They're all horrible to it!" Drina mourned.

"No, not altogether. I've seen far worse notices than these. Here's a good one, praising it quite highly. And another. And here's someone who says:

"'We should have known that thirteen-year-old Drina Adams was a trained dancer even if we had not been told on the programme that she is from the Igor Dominick Ballet School. Her acting patently lacks experience, but she danced charmingly and with feeling. Have we perhaps looked for the first time on one of our future ballerinas?'"

Drina gulped and her eyes blazed.

"Oh, *Grandfather*! Did someone really say that? Oh, I *never* expected – I forgot they'd say things about me. One of our future ballerinas! Oh, it may never be true, but I love him for saying so!"

She ate her breakfast with a warm feeling at her heart. Perhaps it was not, after all, so very bad. Quite a lot of these highly critical people seemed to like the play, and one totally unknown man had actually written that about her. "One of our future ballerinas!" Even if it never came true the words were very sweet.

It had snowed quite heavily in the night and the buildings of Westminster were still touched with dazzling whiteness as Drina ran to Parliament Square to catch her bus. The wind was bitterly cold, but she scarcely noticed it. The snow had somehow given London an extra touch of magic, though it had already turned to slush in the streets.

She met Rose coming out of Holborn tube station and they ran on together, Drina breathlessly telling a little about the previous night. But she did not mention the newspapers.

But it was evident that quite a number of people had read some, at least, of the notices, for when she reached the Dominick School there were many comments.

"We're all going to ask our parents to take us to see you," said Jill, who, though she was Queenie's friend, was not of a jealous nature. "In my case it's my aunt, of course, but she won't mind. She loves the theatre. It must be really thrilling, Drina! And did you see what was said about your being one of our future ballerinas?"

"The man in *The Times* thought the play was awful," said Queenie sourly. "I don't suppose it'll run for long."

But Drina scarcely heard. She was busy fastening her shoes for the ballet class. Once in the Dominick School, the only thing that really mattered was being on time for classes and doing well at her dancing.

Miss Martin greeted her with warm friendliness.

"I see you got some good notices, Drina, though opinion's divided about the play. Congratulations!"

And then Drina, flushed and pleased, ran to the *barre* and lost herself in her work.

Life was very crowded just then at the Dominick School, and as the days passed she thought little about the play. But each evening she went back into the world of the theatre and was Francoise again for a short while. Once the play had opened, she did not see nearly so much of the cast, for she arrived after the play started and left before it finished, but people sometimes dropped into her dressing-room and Lally was always friendly.

"It *may* run," she said once, when they met in a passage, "in spite of the cracks it took from some critics. I'm just keeping my fingers crossed and hoping. Christmas ought to help."

"Oh, I hope it does!" Drina cried, but she could

hardly imagine the play *not* running. After a week or two, it was part of her life and she could not visualise the time coming when she would not whisk in through the stage door of the Queen Elizabeth Theatre, being greeted by the friendly old doorkeeper and smelling the familiar air back stage.

Exams came and passed at the Dominick School and she thought that she had done quite well. The medical examinations passed, too, and everyone seemed pleased with her, but there were some tragedies. One or two girls had foot trouble; one had strained her back and had been trying to carry on without confessing. Several were told that they were not, after all, suitable for one reason or another to continue with their ballet training.

"Something's always hanging over us," said Rose, over whom the doctor had muttered for a long time. "She said I'm anaemic or something, and I'm to have a special diet and go to bed especially early in the holidays."

"But you're all right, really, aren't you?" Drina asked anxiously, staring at the pale cheeks and wide grey eyes of her friend.

"I s'pose so. I've just got to be. I'd die if they threw me out, now."

Rehearsals for *The Golden Fawn* had been going on steadily for some weeks, and Drina found to her great pleasure that she would be able to stay for the greater part of the matinée. Her own early performance was not until 5.30. She had booked two seats for herself and her grandmother and was looking forward eagerly to seeing her friends dance.

The Dominick Theatre was crowded with parents and friends on that Saturday afternoon, and Drina, sitting in front of the Royal Circle, waited eagerly for the curtain to go up. She thought of all the dancers getting dressed and made up without any envy, because now backstage was no mystery to her, though she felt that its fascination would never die.

The Dominick School naturally had a very high standard and the whole performance went without a hitch. First came a short ballet danced by some of the senior students, then a long *divertissement*, and finally the charming fairy ballet, *The Golden Fawn*.

It was so enchanting that Drina almost forgot that she knew everyone on the stage. The music was so tuneful, the setting of a woodland glade so bright and delightful, and she had little fault to find with the dancing.

Just for a moment, as all the fawns did their most important dance, she felt a stab of wistfulness, thinking that she might have been down on the stage of the Dominick Theatre, but the feeling passed quickly. After all, there would be other matinées, and not for anything in the world would she have missed being in *Argument in Paris.*

Breaking up day was on December 20th and by then Christmas was very definitely in the air. The big shops were wonderfully decorated and so were some of the main streets. Regent Street at dusk was a fairy stretch, in spite of the great crowds and the roaring traffic, and she loved to be there as the lights sprang out and the decorations floated overhead.

The Christmas tree had arrived in Trafalgar Square, though it was not immediately provided with its lights, and there were trees, too, in St Martin's and in the Abbey.

Once school had broken up Drina was, of course, much more free, and she spent a great deal of time wandering about London, looking at the Christmas wonders and delighted with all she saw. London, surely, was the loveliest place in the world at Christmas?

She and Rose wandered through the Abbey at dusk on Christmas Eve and saw that the Crib was already in place, and they went to Westminster Cathedral, too, and saw the Crib there. Drina always found the Cathedral very awe-inspiring, with its glittering candles and its wonderful silver mosaics. But she really preferred the Abbey, because it was so old and so drowned in history.

There was all the excitement of receiving parcels, and of course she had to send off several of her own. She had found it hard to find time for shopping that year, but there was a new farming book for Jenny and a pretty scarf for Mrs Pilgrim.

Jenny sent her a new ballet book and a small doll dressed as a dancer, with stiff pink skirts and a pink ribbon holding back her black hair.

"I hope she's like you in the play," Jenny wrote on her Christmas card. "Mother dressed her and I thought she could join Hansl in your dressing-room. Oh, Drina, I *am* looking forward to seeing you again!"

That year, of course, Drina could not go with her grandfather to sing carols round the tree in Trafalgar Square, for every night found her at the theatre. But she did not regret it. She loved every moment of each evening, and it seemed the most natural thing in the world to be Francoise for a short time, dancing on the bright stage before the dark auditorium, where she could catch a blurred glimpse of faces and white programmes. She realised dimly that the theatre was sometimes not very full, but the front stalls were always crowded and she did not think much about it.

On Christmas Eve, she was at the Queen Elizabeth

Theatre as usual, and she and Miss Thorne went home in a taxi through a slight scattering of snow. Drina's heart lifted, because it would be lovely if it would really turn into a white Christmas. As they passed Trafalgar Square, the crowd was still singing round the tree and just for a moment she heard them, for the taxi was held up.

"See amid the winter's snow,
Born to us on earth below –"

"Christmas! How lovely!" thought Drina, huddling into her warm, hooded coat, and she remembered the previous Christmas Eve, when, at the back of her pleasure, had been so many feelings of doubt and guilt. Then she had been practising her dancing without her grandparents' knowledge, and had never believed that they would ever let her go to a ballet school.

"Christmas isn't what it was," said Miss Thorne, with a sigh. She felt old and cold, and she had taken so many children home from theatres in her time that the business was little more than a necessary job to her, though she was fond of Drina and proud of her in a way.

"It's heavenly!" said Drina and, looking at her bright face, the elderly woman felt a stab. It was suddenly strange to be with Betsy Chester's daughter, though the daughter bore so little physical resemblance to the mother. But the spirit was the same. Betsy, too, had been a sensitive child, deeply affected by all that went on around her, always moved by beauty to what had sometimes seemed an unreasonable extent.

There *was* a slight dusting of snow on Christmas morning and the bright world seemed filled with bells. Drina opened her presents from her grandparents before breakfast, and was very thrilled with them. Her grandfather had given her some opera glasses and a pair of fur-lined gloves, and her grandmother produced a large dress-box.

"I'm sure I hope it'll fit you, Drina, but no doubt we can have it altered a little if necessary."

"It" was a scarlet dress, and Drina was enchanted, for her white one was growing shabby. With the dress were silver evening slippers and a tiny silver bag.

"You only need a chance to wear them!" said Mr Chester, and Drina answered happily:

"I shan't be able to wear the dress at Covent Garden, of course, but I am going to some parties. Oh, Granny, it's the loveliest dress I've ever had! Thank you *very* much!"

Christmas Day was rather a quiet time, but very pleasant. Drina and her grandfather went to the Abbey in the morning and walked in the park for a while afterwards, and in the afternoon Drina read Jenny's ballet book, which was one she had been longing to be able to buy. Early in the evening Jenny telephoned, and afterwards they watched the television.

"How lovely to think that Jenny will be here on the 4th!" said Drina, as she kissed her grandparents before going to bed. "I do want her to see *Argument*, though I know she'd sooner have that new film at the Odeon."

"She can have both," said Mrs Chester.

So the time passed happily until New Year's Eve, when Drina went off to the theatre as usual. The slight snow had turned to frost and the night sky was covered with brilliant stars, though it was not easy to see them until Drina stood for a moment in the dark little street where the stage door was.

Everything seemed just as usual and she went cheerfully to her dressing-room, to find Bernadette already there. She was just changing into her practice clothes when the first act ended, and Lally suddenly bounced in. One look at her face and Drina knew that something was wrong.

"What's happened?" she asked anxiously, with visions of someone ill or late.

"Happened? The notice is going up, that's all. We're finishing."

Drina stared at her blankly, one leg in her tights.

"*Finishing*?"

"Yes, on the 11th. It's no surprise, I suppose, but it comes hard."

"But – but – it *can't* finish so soon!"

"Oh, can't it, my child? It's been losing thousands. Didn't you know?"

"No, I – I didn't," and Drina struggled to take in the news. Then her thoughts were immediately for Lally. "Oh, I'm so terribly sorry! And you were going to settle down and enjoy yourself."

"I'll have to find something else. I might get some film work to tide me over. It's all part of the game." Lally shrugged and went off.

The news had jerked Drina out of a dream world into sharp reality, and when Lally had gone she felt deeply miserable. The play had grown to seem a part of life and soon it would end. Even before she was due back at the Dominick School.

And yet, when she stood in the wings waiting for her first cue, all seemed to be as usual. A laugh rippled round the theatre at Marla's exit line. Cecile and her artist friend were carrying on with their scene as they had done every night since the play opened. And Francoise was there, too, fresh from her ballet practice. It all seemed very odd and strange to Drina.

"I never thought it would run," said Miss Thorne,

as they went back to the flat. "I'm sure it's a disappointment to you, but there it is. I must admit, though, that it's hard coming on New Year's Eve."

Mr and Mrs Chester received the news quietly, and perhaps the latter was a good deal relieved, though she was very kind to Drina. She insisted that she must go to bed and not wait up to see the New Year in, and Drina went sadly to her own room. Once in bed, she shed a few tears. It seemed so very sad and such a waste. A play was created; endless trouble went into the scenery, the costumes, to every movement and gesture on the stage. Something became real night after night, and then it was over – finished, and people forgot all about it. Just one of the many West End failures and that was that. Another play would go on at the Queen Elizabeth.

She was still lying there, wide awake, when she heard the first chime of Big Ben and she leapt out of bed, dragging on her dressing-gown and pushing her feet into slippers. The New Year! She stood by her window, seeing the dark river and hearing the bells and hooters, and suddenly her unhappiness fell from her.

"How feeble you were, Drina Adams!" she told herself. "I know you weren't only thinking about yourself, but have some gumption, as Jenny would say. It's been a gorgeous experience and you'll never forget it, and now you'll be able to give your whole time to your dancing again. The Dominick is what matters; you know it is. And someone *did* say that about one of our future ballerinas."

Her last thoughts as she grew warm again in bed, were:

"And you've still got till the 11th. Enjoy every moment of it while you can."

# 7

# The Curtain Falls

Strangely enough, Drina did enjoy the remaining performances of the play. Perhaps it was her knowledge that she must live every moment while she could, but she was very happy during those last days. And she was aware that the other members of the cast seemed to be putting every ounce of effort into their parts. It was some comfort to their pride when a critic wrote in one of the Sunday newspapers:

"*Argument in Paris* finishes its run at the Queen Elizabeth Theatre on the 11th and it might be as well to try to see this unbalanced but well acted play while there is still time. It has failed, and yet there have been memorable moments in it. Lally Devine's performance seems to have increased in power. She seems to me a very promising young actress, with the world before her."

Drina was very glad for Lally and more pleased still when she learned that she had got a part in a new revue. It was not a very big part, but it was something.

So by the time that Drina went to Paddington to meet Jenny, she was quite resigned to the play coming to an end, though Jenny herself was loud in her commiserations.

"It's a dreadful shame! I think you're being very

brave about it. But at least I can see it first."

"It's far worse for the others," said Drina soberly. "Though Lally's got another part, and Bernadette's going to Liverpool to be one of twenty pantomime fairies. Someone's ill – really ill – and several have got colds, so she's going to be in the show, not just an understudy. I'm glad of that, though I don't think she really enjoys the theatre much. She often said she wasn't typical."

"I *can* see it, can't I?" Jenny repeated.

"Oh, of course. Grandfather's got tickets for tomorrow night. He and Granny are seeing it again, too."

It was wonderful to be with Jenny again, and Drina realised that there was no one like her. She was fond of Rose, but there was something real and enduring between herself and Jenny. Jenny was taller, and even, perhaps, a little plumper, but otherwise she had not altered. She poured out all the Willerbury gossip and listened avidly to Drina's news, too, and it was quite hard to have to get ready to go to the theatre. But Jenny assured her that she would be quite happy, and Mrs Chester said that, in any case, the visitor should go to bed early after her long journey.

The next day, which was very cold, they went to Madam Tussaud's and then met Mrs Chester in Regent Street for tea. Afterwards Jenny was very excited to think of going to the theatre.

"I like plays much better than ballet," she informed Drina. "And I've seen so very few. If Mother had wanted me to be an actress instead of a dancer, I think I might have gone through with it, though I do see that it's an awful life in some ways. I wouldn't be your Bernadette, in digs in some Liverpool back street with nineteen other poor kids. Anyway, I'm sure I shall enjoy *Argument* and it will be positively uncanny to see you being Francoise.

"Sometimes it is almost uncanny," Drina admitted, rather shyly. "I just know what Francoise felt like and I'm almost sure that Paris is really outside."

"Then you must be a born actress as well as a dancer."

"I'm not. I don't want to be. It's just that Francoise wants to be a dancer, too, and I know how she feels. If I had to choose between dancing and people I think it would have to be dancing."

"It sounds rather ruthless," said Jenny, eyeing her with a mixture of amusement and respect.

"It sounds awful. But I believe I should."

"Well, you never will have to choose. Or at any rate not until someone wants to marry you. Someone quite ordinary, who works in the provinces or something."

Drina gazed at her, appalled.

"Well, I shouldn't marry the silly man, then. I shan't marry at all."

"Your mother did."

"Yes-s. Well, I don't think I shall. Not until I'm old, anyway; thirty or more. And perhaps no one will ask me."

"They'll ask," said Jenny cheerfully. "How could they fail to, you silly idiot? Still, you needn't worry yet. And if I have any say in *my* life I shall marry a farmer and have six children and there'll be no difficulty at all."

"Granny always says that dancers lead unnatural lives," Drina remarked. "I believe she'd like me to marry a farmer, too."

"Well, you never will – *that's* certain enough," said Jenny. "But I'm not so sure about the businessman from the provinces."

"Well, I *am!*" said Drina roundly, and then what she considered as a silly and profitless conversation came to an end.

Jenny *did* enjoy the play and very much admired Drina.

"You nearly made me cry. In fact, I had a large tear wobbling about all the time, but I knew your granny would be dreadfully shocked if I let it fall. And I think Marla Lerieu was *beautiful*, but terribly hard and unkind."

"She isn't really; that was just the part. She's sweet." said Drina, as they drank hot milk and ate biscuits very late.

The last few performances of the play seemed to come and go very quickly, and finally it was the last performance of all. The theatre was fairly well booked and Drina thought rebelliously that it seemed silly not to keep on, but presumably the people who had backed the play knew best.

She felt sad as she danced for the last time, and perhaps it lent an extra touch of pathos to Francoise's final exit. At any rate, quite a burst of applause followed her.

She had said goodbye to everyone in the interval and there was nothing to do but pack her things and take a last look round the little dressing-room.

"I don't suppose I shall ever, ever have one again until I'm grown up."

"You never know, dear!" said Miss Thorne.

"Well, I don't think it's a bit likely. Even if I ever dance in the *corps de ballet* I shall have to share with a lot of others."

In spite of Jenny's presence Drina did feel slightly depressed the next day, which was a Sunday, but by the Monday she had cheered up, because it was impossible to be dismal for long when the sun was shining again and Jenny was so patently bent on enjoying every moment in London.

At lunch-time Mr Chester telephoned and Drina, who had answered the phone, was thrilled to hear that he had got four tickets for the Festival Ballet that night.

"Covent Garden and the Dominick are fully booked, but a friend of mine in the office says I can have his tickets and he'll go to the Festival Hall another night. You've never seen the Festival Company, Drina, and I believe they're very good."

"I'd *love* it!" Drina cried. "What are they doing?"

"Oh, *Les Sylphides*, and part of *Swan Lake*, *Alice in Wonderland* – the whole of it, and I believe it's quite a long ballet – and *Napoli*."

"Oh, I'd love to see *Napoli*, especially!" Drina said happily. "It's Italian; I've heard about it. And fancy *Alice*! Oh, thank you, Grandfather!"

"You can put on your new scarlet dress. It's a good excuse for dressing up."

So Drina and Jenny dressed after tea, with much conversation and running from one room to another. Jenny had at last managed to persuade her mother that pale blue made her look too fat, and her new dress was a soft, dull green, which suited her fair colouring very well.

Mr Chester drove them to the Festival Hall and Jenny cried, as they crossed Westminster Bridge:

"Oh, I do adore London!"

"But you wouldn't like to live here, would you?" Mrs Chester asked, laughing.

"No, thank you," Jenny answered very firmly. "But I love it at times like this."

"Even when we're going to the ballet?" said Drina slyly.

"Oh, I've told you before. I don't mind the ballet now that I haven't got to bother about it. Besides, I like modern ones like *Alice* and I've heard of the Italian one. I don't like the droopy ones, all romantic music and waving arms."

"Oh, Jenny!" Drina protested, assuming correctly that her friend was visualising *Les Sylphides*. "And I do love it so. I don't think I could ever get tired of it. The music is beautiful, and the arms –"

The argument came to an end because they had to leave the car then, and Drina was too happy, as they found their seats, to start it again. She loved *Les Sylphides*, but Jenny thought it "droopy". That was one of the differences between them, but it didn't really matter. And Jenny was too good a theatregoer, in any case, to do other than sit perfectly still during any ballet, however much it bored her.

*Les Sylphides*, as usual, opened the programme, and Drina was immediately transported with the dancers into the moonlit glade. She had seen the ballet twice before – once on that long ago occasion at the Grand Theatre, Willerbury, and once at Covent Garden – but every moment, every change of the music was still a delight.

*Alice in Wonderland* was as different as it could be – an absolutely modern ballet. She enjoyed it, especially the Mad Hatter's Tea-Party and the Lobster Quadrille, but it had not the magic for her of classical ballet.

But the *pas de deux* from *Swan Lake* filled her with enchantment again. Such beautiful, effortless movement! Would *she* ever be able to dance like that in a thousand years? She watched the famous thirty-two *fouettés* with bated breath and shining eyes and at the end clapped so wildly that her hands hurt for some time afterwards.

*Napoli*, with its beautiful backcloth of the Bay of Naples, delighted her, for it was so vivid and colourful. And even Jenny was sitting forward in her seat during the Tarantella.

"Ballet!" thought Drina, during the last moments. "There's nothing else really. The play was interesting and I loved being Francoise, but I want to dance. I want to learn and learn and get into the Dominick *corps de ballet*."

As they drove back along the Embankment, she sat back feeling warm and deeply happy. In two days' time she would go back to the Dominick School and work would start again.

"I suppose you feel that a lot has happened since last

year?" said Jenny, later, and Drina cried:

"Oh, yes! Some of it was rather awful, of course. When I first went to the Dominick I wasn't very good, and I was so scared that they'd throw me out. It all got on top of me for a while. But then I went to Switzerland and after that things were different. I think I've learned a lot, and my dancing has improved."

"And then there was the play."

"Yes," said Drina soberly. "I shall never forget that, but it wasn't really part of it. It was an extra experience. This year, I shall just work hard and dance."